"BOUND BY DESIRE"

SILENCE IN THE Storm

Kaunas 2024

BOUND BY DESIRE

Silence in the Storm

Published by Silence in the Storm, 2024.

BOUND BY DESIRE

First edition. October 30, 2024.

Copyright © 2024 Silence in the Storm.

ISBN: 979-8227646828

Written by Silence in the Storm.

Table of Contents

"Always be kind, have a little courage and always believe in small miracles."
Cinderella

Mona

As I observed the table set for the festive gathering, I sensed him standing behind me. He wrapped his arms around me, placing his hands gently on my stomach. His warm lips brushed against my ear as he whispered softly:

"Don't worry, everything will be fine. You'll see."

I sighed. We were the first to arrive at his parents' house. His entire family was supposed to gather here, and he was about to introduce me as his future wife. I felt tense. After all, today would determine whether they would accept me as part of their family. But the sound of shattering glass somewhere in the distance pulled me back into memories I had long tried to forget.

Three months ago

I was kneeling on the ground, tears streaming down my face, begging him:

"Please, listen to me..."

But Jeremy looked at me with disdain, stepping back as if I were diseased. Then, arrogantly pulling out his wallet, he tossed a thousand euros onto the table.

"Here, for your effort in "servicing" me. You can use it to get rid of "his" child."

"That's not true! she lied to you!" I screamed through my tears, unable to see him clearly.

"Why would she lie?" he laughed mockingly. "Did you think you'd pass off your bastard as mine?"

"Jeremy, it's not true," I tried to stop him.

"I loved you so much," I saw the pain in his eyes. "And you... You're nothing but a whore!"

He slammed his fist on the table so hard that the glass jumped, fell to the ground, and shattered into countless pieces—just like my heart. His shouted words rang in my ears, and inside, I felt completely hollow. Through my tears, I looked at the man I loved, unable to comprehend why he was doing this.

"And don't even think about trying to find me. Tomorrow, I'm terminating the lease. You have until tonight to pack up and leave this apartment," he said, slamming the door as he left.

He left without listening to me, without giving me a chance to explain. He just shut the door on our shared life, which had lasted two years.

Everything has a beginning and an end.

I don't remember how long I lay there crying, nor how I managed to get up. But I will never forget the image of the money he had thrown on the table or his words telling me to get rid of "his" child.

How did I end up in Paris? God, it's like a twisted version of Cinderella's story.

I was born in a small town in Lithuania, the second child in the family. A family? Hardly. My mother never let me forget that my arrival was the greatest misfortune of her life, ruining her happiness and taking away her beloved husband—my older sister Daiva's loving father. Apparently, it was my fault that she spread her legs for some soldier and got pregnant. And when I was born, it became clear that I looked nothing like her, perfect Daiva, or her adoring father. God, I was born just to take happiness and love away from these kind and wonderful people.

All my life, I envied my older sister. Her beautiful, wavy blonde hair, her flawless face, her perfect body. She was my mother's favorite child. It was wonderful to have a child who excelled in school, danced so beautifully, and behaved so perfectly. I envied her for the attention she got from boys, for her many friends. I was nearly four years younger than her, a skinny girl with pale skin, dark hair, and slightly slanted blue eyes—a strange combination. By the time I was twelve, I had already outgrown Daiva in height. Of course, her hand-me-down clothes no longer fit me, which didn't please my mother. But I preferred to have my two pairs of jeans rather than a pile of worn-out clothes from my sister.

All my life, I tried to prove to my mother that I wasn't worse than her precious Daiva. I was the child who could do it all: needed someone to run? I ran. Needed someone to dance? I danced. Needed someone to recite poetry? here I was. And I studied so well that it was hard for Daiva to compete with me. But...

But by the time I was in ninth grade, I realized one thing: only Daiva could go to university. The child who ruined her life had no such opportunities.

I remember the day she told me that very clearly. Believe me, for a child to understand something like that is a heavy burden. That day, sitting under an old oak tree and gazing at the moon, I swore to the world that I would do everything in my power to escape this miserable place, and one day, somehow, I would achieve my goals and prove to her that I wasn't worse than the "amazing" Daiva.

My best friend Cornelia lived in a completely different world than I did.

We had been friends since the seventh grade when her father moved to our town and started his own company. We were inseparable. Her parents wanted her to study medicine, but Cora dreamed of becoming a world-class model. And to be fair, Cora was beautiful. No, perhaps "very" beautiful. We shared a secret dream: after school, we would escape together to Paris. She would become a model, and I would find some job there. And after that? well, even Cora didn't know what would come next. I was always afraid that if I said it out loud, the dream wouldn't come true.

It wasn't difficult for Cora to leave for Paris. But I had no one to support me. So, I saved every penny, working after school and throughout the summers. I took on jobs I never mentioned to anyone, no matter the cost. All that mattered was one thing: getting out of there.

Time passed. I noticed how men looked at me. I wasn't a perfect beauty like Daiva, but I never lacked male attention. They called me an "exotic beauty". But men weren't my goal. I longed to go to America and become... well, we'll get to that later.

So, our escape plan worked. Cora disappointed her family. Or maybe she didn't—she had been accepted into medical academy, but she didn't start her studies that year. As for me, my departure didn't disappoint anyone. I just left a note thanking them for raising me. I had no intention of returning. I'd rather die than go back and prove that I was a failure.

We found a small room in Montmartre with a single wide bed and grand ambitions to conquer the world. But as they say, "man plans, and god laughs." On the second day of our stay, in a small pizzeria, a photographer approached us, offering me the chance to do a photoshoot because, in his words, I was an extraordinary, exceptionally beautiful girl who could achieve great things in life.

I still remember the look on Cora's face when he said that. I wasn't picky—I needed work. And if those photos could give me the funds to survive, why not? I loved the camera, and it loved me. I could play any role in front of it. Want a perfect seductress? done. Need an innocent orphan? I'm your girl. I had never truly been myself my whole life. Pretending to be someone else was something I had learned from my mother. I could be anyone I wanted to be. And those photos helped me. Jacques worked for a prestigious agency as a photographer, and soon I was working full-time. The photos turned out so beautiful that I wanted to send them home. But I didn't.

Before long, I started flying around the world for photoshoots.

As for Cora, she didn't land her dream job. But I managed to get her a position at the agency where I worked. She helped with clothes and other tasks there.

How did Jeremy come into my life?

About three months later, we moved into a one-room apartment. Since I was rarely home, Cornelia usually had the place to herself. If there was one thing she didn't lack, it was men in her life. One day, after returning from south Korea, where I had been for about three weeks, I found him in my room. Cornelia was over the moon after meeting him, and they had been enjoying each other's company for a good two weeks. I didn't have much time for men, so that evening I joined them for dinner, though Jeremy had also invited his friend to join us.

That night, Jeremy couldn't take his eyes off me. After the second bottle of champagne, I realized that I liked him too. But that's where it ended. Cornelia wasn't stupid. That night probably marked the beginning of our rivalry. I wasn't trying to steal Jeremy for myself because I knew that no man would be interested in a girl who spent most of her month traveling the world. I was a realist. It wasn't time for love; I needed money to achieve my dreams.

The second time I met Jeremy was at a party where Cornelia wasn't around. We were celebrating the completion of a campaign, and there were quite a few famous people in attendance. I wasn't looking for a man, but Jeremy stuck to me like glue. We spent the entire evening together. Having monopolized my attention, he didn't let anyone else approach me. And after that, we met a few more times.

Jeremy had his own company in Paris. He wasn't French. Cornelia and I had a big argument because she thought I had deliberately seduced her Jeremy. Then he offered me to move into his apartment. At first, I wasn't sure if it was the right decision, but knowing that he constantly travelled between Amsterdam, Paris, London, and New

York, and I was just a guest in Paris, I agreed. I wasn't fond of relying on others, but when he mentioned that I wouldn't have to pay rent, I was relieved. To be clear, I had my own room in his apartment, and our relationship was purely friendly, meant to satisfy both of our needs. But as time passed, he spent more and more time in Paris, and I was getting more work in Europe rather than in the east. His behavior shifted from friendly to possessive. We got along well, and eventually, we realized that our connection was deeper than friendship. We became a serious couple.

When he got tired of seeing me in magazines and on posters, he selfishly suggested that we move in together and get married. It wasn't a surprise. We were compatible. I found myself falling for him more and more. When he said he wanted to have a child with me, I was overjoyed. But then everything took a different turn. My contract was coming to an end when I realized I was pregnant. And by the time I figured it out, it was too late. The constant starving and heavy workload had affected my cycle, so I hadn't even suspected that I was pregnant. When I finally found out, I knew there was no point in continuing my contract. Jeremy was over the moon.

There were about three months left until Christmas when he came home darker than a storm cloud.

He grabbed my phone and demanded I unlock it, even though he knew the code—he had given me the phone, after all. Surprised by his behavior, I did as he asked. I had nothing to hide from him.

For some reason, a few days earlier, I had received a text from an unknown number. The message said, "Sweetheart, happy little anniversary. I love you so much. Well, both of you." I found it odd, laughed it off, and then forgot to delete it after the doorbell rang and a courier distracted me. Now, Jeremy, like a furious lion, was accusing me of infidelity because of that message. He didn't even let me explain. He said Cornelia had told him that I was too close to Jacques. And that three months ago, when he was out of Paris, she claimed to have seen

Jacques and me hugging outside his house after a party. To top it off, Jeremy added that Jacques had supposedly confided in a friend that I was pregnant.

It all sounded absurd to me. Mostly because Jacques was my only true friend. But Cornelia didn't know that Jacques was gay, and I had never interested him as a woman. That's when I realized she had done this to get back at me. I tried to explain it to Jeremy, but he wasn't listening anymore. And then, it was over.

I was left with one realization: I had no job, no place to live, and the little money I had wouldn't last long. But misfortune never comes alone. My phone rang. When I answered, my agency owner, Victoria, wasn't speaking—she was yelling. She accused me of seducing her husband, Pierre, and promised to ensure I wouldn't get work anywhere again.

What else could I do? I was three months pregnant, homeless, jobless. And my mother had been right all along—I was worthless, unwanted.

I got up from the floor. Jeremy had left some money on the table. No. I couldn't just get rid of the baby. That would be deeply unfair to the child.

In the closet was my only suitcase. I packed everything that was important to me. I knew that by selling my expensive designer clothes, I could survive for a while until I found some work—most likely back in Lithuania.

Before leaving, I wrote Jeremy a letter, explaining the whole truth. Yes, I wanted him to know. After all, the life growing inside me had the right to know who its father was. Unlike me. If Jeremy never reached out, that was his problem. In the letter, I demanded a paternity test after the baby was born, because this was the child Jeremy had wanted, and he wouldn't get away from this responsibility so easily. At that point, I wasn't sure what I felt for him anymore. Disgust, maybe? How could you not feel disgust when you live with someone for two years, and they don't even know you?

I turned to take one last look at the home where I had been so happy. Then, I lifted my head, straightened up, and after slamming the door behind me, I had to admit to myself that things just hadn't worked out.

A journey back to the past

Sitting in the taxi, I couldn't see the road through my tears. It was already night when I reached the airport. My flight was only tomorrow, but what did it matter when you're traveling to nowhere? I bought a one-way ticket. I don't even remember how I ended up at my favorite café, the one where I'd spent so much time before flights. I bought a bottle of sparkling water, sat down, and wiped away my tears. This was how my attempt to change my life ended. Instead, I had completely ruined it.

"Excuse me, miss," I heard a calm male voice.

At first, I didn't realize he was speaking to me. But then I felt someone's hand on mine. Startled, I looked up, wiping my eyes to see who was concerned about me at this hour.

A man sat down beside me. A fine suit, expensive watch, silk tie. My eyes wandered to his face—perhaps thirty-six, maybe older. Thick, blonde hair, perfectly cut. A sharp jawline. Three-day stubble, straight nose, brown eyes. He smelled of good cologne, which made me think he wasn't just an ordinary office worker waiting for a business flight.

"What?" I asked quietly.

"Don't be upset, but when you see a woman crying for two hours straight, you can't help but be concerned. Can I help you?" his calm voice soothed me like a warm breeze.

"Me?" I raised my eyebrows in surprise.

Yes, I was used to male attention, more than enough of it. But I had always been immune to it. Jeremy was my whole world. I loved him; I didn't need anyone else. The strangest part was that this stranger wasn't trying to seduce me like others did. He was just talking.

"Yes, you," he nodded. "I can't stand to see women cry."

I smiled.

"I don't usually cry, but now..." I lowered my eyes, struggling to even speak.

"What happened?"

I tilted my head back to stop the tears from spilling.

"You know," I laughed, "my whole world collapsed today."

He chuckled.

"So, you're washing away the pain with sparkling water?"

I smiled faintly.

"Some pain can't be washed away."

"I know," he nodded. "But time heals."

"I don't think so," I sighed. "You know, I spent my whole life trying to achieve more than I could. I worked so hard, put in so much effort. And in one moment, I lost everything I had worked for."

"Oh," he sighed. "But you're so young, such a beautiful woman."

I snorted.

"That doesn't matter. Neither beauty nor youth. It hurts when the people you love, the ones you trusted unconditionally, betray you..." I sighed again, wiping more tears from my face.

"Believe me, I know that feeling well," he chuckled, but there was sadness in his voice.

"And how do you cope? does time really heal it?" I asked, genuinely curious.

He shook his head slowly.

"It's been three years, and I still think I wasn't good enough, not worthy enough. That's why I was left behind."

"See? For men, it's much easier. You just turn around, close the door behind you, and walk away to someone else."

He sighed again.

"Sometimes women do that too—close the door and move on to someone else."

Now it was my turn to sigh.

"Did you have a fight with your boyfriend?" he asked softly.

"No, I didn't even have a chance to. He just came in, declared that our two years together were a mistake, accused me of things I didn't do, and left, after insulting me."

"Maybe he'll come to his senses and return? By the way, when's your flight?"

"Tomorrow," I laughed.

"So, what are you doing here?" he seemed surprised.

"I have nowhere else to go," I replied sadly, lowering my head.

"Come on, I know a great place in the VIP lounge to have a glass of wine," he said, trying to stand up and encourage me to follow.

I shook my head and turned my face toward the balcony.

"I can't drink anymore," I whispered, burying my face in my hands. "He left us."

"Us?" he looked confused.

"I'm pregnant..." I said it out loud, not sure if I was saying it to myself or to the world. I didn't know who I was speaking to anymore.

He sat back down beside me.

"He left you while you're pregnant?" his brow furrowed in disbelief.

I laughed at the absurdity of my situation.

"He wanted this child, and then he just claimed it wasn't his..." I trailed off, not able to finish the sentence, and turned my gaze away.

"My god. Is he right?" I felt his hand gently on my shoulder.

I laughed bitterly.

"The baby is his, but he believed my friend instead of me. She was getting back at me for old grievances."

"That's awful," he whispered softly. "Come on, this isn't the best place to spend the night."

"You know, this place suits me just fine. I'm going back home to let everyone see, once again, that I'm a failure in life. Just to confirm that someone like me can never have a normal life," I lowered my head, trying to hide the despair in my eyes.

"Enough feeling sorry for yourself. Get up, let's get out of here," he said, trying to lift me by my elbow.

"Where?" I asked, surprised.

"Anywhere. It doesn't matter. I can't leave you here. Everyone deserves a second chance in life."

I laughed.

"People like me don't get second chances."

"Look at me," he said quietly.

I shook my head.

"Look at me," he now demanded.

Curious about what he wanted; I lifted my eyes.

"Do you trust me?" he asked, his face serious.

I chuckled.

"No. I don't even trust myself anymore."

"That's not good. Let's go."

"Where?" I asked again.

"I have a meeting with someone. They'll be arriving in half an hour."

"And?"

"After that, I'll show you your second chance."

"Sir, I'm not that kind of woman," I laughed softly.

"What are you talking about?" he asked, raising an eyebrow.

"I'm serious, and..." I tried to explain that I wouldn't sleep with him if that was his plan.

"Oh..." he laughed. "You know, when I was at my lowest, someone reached out and helped me. When I wanted to repay them, they simply told me that the time would come for me to help someone else in need. I think that time has come."

I raised my eyebrows in surprise.

"Sir, I don't believe in fairy tales anymore," I laughed.

"Then start believing. Where's your stuff?"

I nodded toward a small suitcase.

"See? my whole life fits in there."

"That's great. I don't like to travel with too much stuff."

"And where are you going?" I asked, curious.

"To show you a fairy tale," he laughed. "Tell me, do you absolutely have to fly tomorrow?"

I shook my head.

"Great. Let's return your ticket."

He grabbed my suitcase, took my hand, and led me like a child.

And yes, he met the person who handed him a briefcase, and then he cheerfully said:

"Let's go. By the way, do you happen to have a valid US Visa?"

I nodded.

"I have all kinds of visas, many of them."

"You look familiar," he furrowed his brow.

I laughed.

"No wonder," I replied.

"Want to give me a hint?"

I nodded toward a large advertisement on the wall, where I was modelling luxury lingerie.

He stopped, took a good look at the ad, then glanced back at me, and then at the poster again.

"You look even better in real life," he winked.

"Where are we going?" I still tried to figure out his plans for me.

"To my car. Private planes don't take off from here," he shrugged.

"And where are we flying?" I asked, intrigued.

"Maybe on vacation. Or maybe to start a new chapter of your life. It depends on how you look at it."

"And what's my role in this play?"

"That's entirely up to you," he winked again.

"Let's get one thing straight—I'm not offering anything intimate, okay?" I tried to set boundaries.

"But will you at least keep me company?"

"Of course," I smiled.

"You know, I don't expect anything anymore," he said calmly.

"Why? you're not that old."

"No, but..."

"But what?" I stopped, wanting to learn more about who I was dealing with.

He lowered his eyes.

"Well, I've told you everything. You don't know me. What's there to be afraid of? You'll tell me, and I'll forget."

Mona

We reached the exit, and he pulled out his phone, made a call, and ordered someone to come pick us up. Then he turned to me.

"I'll explain in the car."

A black limousine arrived.

He tossed the suitcase into the trunk, opened the door for me, and got in from the other side. Oh my, everything inside looked so luxurious. He pressed a button, and the window separating the driver from us closed.

"Well..." I encouraged him to start.

"I know the taste of betrayal very well. My woman left me, betraying me with my business competitor. She didn't just take my heart with her; she also took valuable information."

"Oh..."

"And that's not all. She destroyed our child, claiming I wasn't worthy of having children with her."

"Oh my god, that's terrible," I furrowed my brows. "But wait, I have something to tell you," I felt very uncomfortable. "I'm not a kept woman. I've worked hard as a model all this time. Right now, I can't afford to be extravagant because I'll have to find a way to support my child in a country I haven't lived in for a long time. So, if where we're going is expensive, I'll must decline the trip."

He looked at me quietly and asked, "answer me one question," he paused, seeming deep in thought. "No, maybe two."

I leaned back.

"Do you like me, even a little?"

Not understanding the point of the question, I furrowed my brows. "I can't judge a person after talking for half an hour. As a man, you're charming. You're easy to talk to."

"Good. How long have you been pregnant?"

"I won't agree to terminate the pregnancy," I shook my head. "Three months."

"Perfect. Then I'm offering you a deal."

"Oh god," I sighed. I knew something was off. "Stop the car, I want to get out."

"No, you misunderstood," he now shook his head. "I'm offering you to live with me. I will take care of you and the baby. You won't need to go back where you don't want to. You can do whatever you wish, and I'll consider the child my own."

"Are you out of your mind?" I laughed. "What do you get out of this?"

"First, I won't have to hire someone to pretend to be my partner. Second, I'll have an extraordinary woman living under my roof, and I'll care for the child I lost in my life. That's more than enough for me."

"But wait, aren't you afraid I'll rob you, run away, or do something crazy?"

"No, I'm good at reading people, and what I've seen so far is enough. You'll be perfect for me."

"So, will you prepare some sort of contract for me to sign?" I frowned.

"Oh god, no. Why? you'll have all the conditions for your personal life—your own room, your own driver, a nanny for the child, and whatever else you need."

"I see, but I still feel like you're about to say 'but...' what do you expect from me?"

He smiled and looked down. "You see, I travel a lot. I own a large company that operates in many countries. I need a woman by my side who will travel with me, look happy, and represent me and my family."

"I understand. What else?"

"I'm a loner. I enjoy peace, and I spend a lot of time on an island. I don't like noisy parties, unnecessary publicity, or chaos."

"Which island do you live on?" I asked, surprised.

"A small one, in the Bahamas. My own island."

"You own an island?" I think my jaw dropped.

He nodded. "It's not big, but it's private."

"So, you're really rich?" I laughed.

"Depends on what you consider wealth."

"Don't take offense, but I don't have anyone in my circle who's as wealthy as you."

He waved his hand dismissively.

"But you do understand that small children can be noisy. Won't we bother you?" I asked, unsure.

"No, the child will be mine. How could they bother me? the house is large, and if I need silence, I'll find a place to work. It's beautiful and peaceful there, perfect for raising a child."

"And in terms of safety? if you live there alone, don't you get visitors?"

"There's security for that."

"Jesus," I sighed, leaning back into the seat. "You know, I've learned to be responsible for myself, but why do I feel like I'm diving headfirst into some crazy adventure?"

"Relax, you don't have to worry about anything. I'll do the thinking. You just need to relax and enjoy life."

"But... you know... I... You need to know that I need time to get to know someone, and I can't promise that I'll jump into your arms the moment we arrive."

"Oh, I totally forgot to ask your name," he shrugged.

I burst out laughing.

"Didn't I tell you this is madness? my name is Mona."

"Mona?"

"Yes, yes, like Mona Lisa."

"I'm Erik," he smiled warmly.

"Nice to meet you. Erik, I'm a calm person. We won't do anything you don't want to. I'll respect your wishes."

"But Erik, you don't even know me. I don't even know if you really like me."

"So what? I knew Rachel very well and look how that turned out."

"All right..." I sighed and leaned back. "If I told anyone about this, they'd think I'm crazy."

"Just relax; you don't need to worry about anything."

"I feel like I'm dreaming," I laughed.

"So, do I. After all, it's not every day you acquire a wife and a child in an hour."

Now we were both laughing together.

"So, what were you doing in Paris?" I asked him. "Do you live there?"

"No, I was flying from Tokyo. We landed here because I needed to pick up documents from my trustee, who flew in from London. I plan to stay on the island until Christmas."

"Oh, so you live elsewhere as well?" I asked, intrigued.

"Yes, I have places in Tokyo, Hong Kong, London, Madrid, Geneva, nice, New York, Las Vegas, Ottawa, and a few other spots."

"You have so many houses?" I asked, shocked.

"No, I only have homes in the US. And on the island. The other places are just good apartments. It's not worth having houses where I only stay briefly."

"Jesus," I laughed.

"What do you like to do in your free time?" I asked him.

"In my free time?" he furrowed his brows. "I like sailing, swimming, diving. Reading books, listening to good music. I enjoy cooking."

"You're the perfect man," I laughed. "I don't cook because I barely eat."

"You'll need to change that habit. You're pregnant."

"Listen, but if it's an isolated island and I need medical help?" I started to worry.

"We'd fly to the mainland," he laughed. "If it would make you feel better, when the time comes closer, I'll hire medical staff to live with us."

"You're starting to grow on me," I smiled at him.

"And I liked you from the moment I saw you in that café. What do you do in your free time?"

"Well, I've never had much free time. I used to go to the gym, run, attend parties, but I've always liked reading."

"What do you read?"

"Everything, but romance novels helped me relax after a hard day's work. What about you?"

"I enjoy science fiction. Detective novels."

"Of course," I waved my hand.

"Then before we fly, we need to stop at a bookstore. I have a huge library, but not a single romance novel."

"I'm sorry, I can't afford to spend money on books," I shook my head.

"As I said, relax, it's my responsibility to take care of you," he pulled out his phone and dialled a number.

"Magda, I need books. Get all the new releases for me and romance novels for my fiancée. Pass them to Michael. Can you do that in an hour? You're wonderful, thanks."

"Wow," I laughed.

"I think I'll have much less time for reading now," he winked.

"And what if you get bored of me?"

"I'll run away," he laughed. "I'll get on a plane and fly off."

"Do you fly it yourself?" he was surprising me more and more.

"Of course, it's such a pleasure," he smiled blissfully.

"Wow," I sighed.

"So now we're flying to the island?"

"No, we're heading to New York. I have a meeting, and then we'll rest. Have you ever been to New York?"

"I've been a couple of times, but just briefly. I don't know the city well."

"Then we'll spend a few days in New York, and I'll show you around."

"Thank you."

"By the way, do you have simple clothes for island life in your suitcase?"

"What do you mean?" I furrowed my brows.

"Hmm... Simple shorts, tops, sandals."

"No, I'm only bringing expensive clothes because selling them at home will help me earn some money," I looked down.

"Great, then we need to get you some casual clothes too."

My stomach growled—I'd completely forgotten to eat with all the nerves and rushing.

"You're hungry," he noted.

I nodded.

"You'll eat on the plane. Next time, tell me. It's not good for you to go hungry."

Jeremy

I was rushing to finish my work and head home. Today is a special day at home—we're celebrating our two-year anniversary. A beautiful bouquet of white lilies is waiting for me on the table, a perfect gift for Mona. My thoughts about her are interrupted by my assistant walking through the door.

"Sir, there's a woman named Cornelia insisting to see you. She says you know her and that she has important news for you."

"Let her in," I mumbled quietly.

Cornelia is an old acquaintance. I owe her for introducing me to Mona. Things didn't turn out so well for Cornelia in the end, but let's be real—Mona is a gem compared to her. The first time I saw Mona, I was captivated. She's exotic, so sexy, and those eyes—I was hooked the moment I saw her. I thought she'd fall for me like all the others. My money, my status—they attract women like honey attracts flies. But Mona wasn't like the others. I couldn't get her the first time. Or the second. Or the third.

She seemed so focused, determined, with some goal I still don't understand. She doesn't talk much, but when she does, it's always something smart. Her body? it's a fortress of sex. No wonder photographers adore her. I'm insanely jealous of the world because of her. Those sultry pictures of her in lingerie are everywhere, and I can only imagine some guy in Korea or Germany drooling over her. When we finally got together and started living together, my happiness knew no bounds. The only problem is that she's incredibly busy. South Korea goes crazy for her. Whenever she's away, I can barely wait for her to return. Sometimes I think her agent over there is in love with her or, at the very least, infatuated. He gets her the best gigs, the top photographers, but she doesn't notice, thank God.

Mona is the light of my life. I adore her. If she agreed, I'd marry her tonight. But Mona doesn't want to commit. Sometimes I feel like she's only working to save up for something. It drives me nuts. I have more than enough money for a good life, but she barely uses it. She lives a minimalist lifestyle, eating little, shopping minimally, and spending next to nothing. So, when I told her I wanted to marry her, she didn't squeal with joy. Instead, she frowned, as if my proposal would distract her from whatever her mysterious goal is.

I know she struggled in that poor country. She didn't get along with her mother either. It's odd, though—I've never heard her speak to her mother all this time. But now I'm on top of the world because I managed to get her pregnant, which means only one thing: she'll stop jetting around the world, stop showing off her body, which I don't want to share with anyone, and she'll marry me. My wife won't work. That's what I'm looking forward to. And I just found out we're expecting a baby a few days ago. She didn't even know. Her irregular cycles used to drive me crazy, but now everything is perfect. She's mine. My fiancée, and after Christmas, she'll be my wife. Next week, we're going on a vacation while she can still travel. For Christmas, I'll take her to meet my family. My brother will be green with envy. Finally, I'll have bested him in something. He's always been smarter, shrewder, and, of course, much richer. After all, we're only half-brothers, sharing the same mother.

Our mother divorced his father long ago, but when his father passed, he left everything to my brother. Now he's a billionaire. But what good has that done him? His wife betrayed him, had an abortion, and ran off with a competitor. Not only that, but she stole the latest product information from our company. He still hasn't recovered. Fool. He should just find some girl and screw around, but no, he's locked himself away, mourning his lost youth. How pathetic. When he sees my gorgeous wife, his billions will pale in comparison.

The door opens, and Cornelia saunters in, hips swaying, glowing like some sex goddess. That's all she's good for—not much more. She's limited, and not the brightest.

"Hey, Jeremy, how are you?" she says.

"I'm in a hurry. Say what you need to, and let's wrap this up," I reply.

She glances at the bouquet, leans in to sniff the lilies, her breasts straining against the low neckline of her blouse.

"Jeremy, if you knew something bad about me, as a friend, would you tell me?" she asks, leaning.

Provocatively against my desk.

Who does she think she is? Glancing at my watch, I respond, "of course, Cornelia, of course."

"So, if I stayed to keep you company, you wouldn't be mad?" she teases.

I frown, not understanding what she's getting at.

"Who are the flowers for?" she asks casually.

"For Mona. We're celebrating our two-year anniversary today."

She snorts, and I find it odd.

"Something funny?" I ask, annoyed.

She sighs, as if carrying a heavy burden on her chest.

"She doesn't deserve those flowers. Jeremy, I'm sorry, but I think you should know that she's been seeing Jacques. They're very close, but you already know that don't you?" She says, dragging out her words, and stopping me in my tracks.

"What are you trying to say?" I frown.

"Come on, Jeremy, don't be so naïve. How do you think she landed that modelling gig here? with so many women more beautiful than her? a plain mouse like her?" Cornelia laughs, adjusting my tie with her fingers.

Her words taste bitter, and I step back from her.

"We both came here together. On the second day, we met Jacques. You know I was supposed to be the model, not her. But she started flirting with Jacques, then spread her legs wide, and voilà—she's a model at a prestigious firm. How do you think she got that position?" Cornelia laughs again. "I don't even know how many men she's slept with to climb up her pedestal."

I felt the air leave the room, loosening my tie as I struggled to breathe.

"You know, Jeremy, I've always adored you. Not like her."

"Why are you saying this?" I ask, confused about what she wants.

"isn't it true that she's pregnant?" she smirks strangely.

I nod.

"How could she not notice she's pregnant for three months?" Cornelia laughs again.

I shoot her a glare.

"Don't be ridiculous, her cycle is irregular," I defend mona.

"God, Jeremy, are you really that naïve?" Cornelia moves closer and brushes her fingers across my cheek. "I would never betray you."

I push her away, agitated.

"What nonsense are you spewing?" I yell.

"The baby is Jacques'. He hesitated for a long time, then dumped both her and the child. She's clever, though. She passed it off as yours. And you really think the baby's yours?" Cornelia laughs again. "The whole agency knows about it."

I could feel the blood boiling in my veins, sweat covering my skin.

"Nonsense, the baby is mine," I refuse to believe the venom coming out of her mouth.

"I wish it were true," she laughs. "Do you remember when you flew to London for a few days?"

"Yes…" I frown, trying to remember.

"When was that?"

I began counting in my head, and it all lined up. I felt the air leave my lungs.

"I don't believe it," I shouted at her.

"You can believe it or not, I don't care. But I don't want someone as wonderful as you, whom I love so much, to be deceived like this."

"Do you have proof?" I demand angrily.

"Of course. She spent two nights at his place after that party while you were away. Do you get it now? she's been cheating on you. I saw it myself; my house is on the way to his. We all took the same bus that was rented for us, and they both got off at his house."

I couldn't listen anymore, but she wasn't finished.

"When I was organizing the clothes for a photo shoot, I saw him texting her. Check her phone if you don't believe me. She's only with you for your money, didn't you see that?" Cornelia whispered in my ear. "she's a total gold digger, how did you not see it?"

"I have to go," I hissed.

"You're not going anywhere alone. I won't let you," she grabbed my elbow. "You can't drive in this state. I'll take you, you talk to her, and I'll wait for you in the car. If things don't go well, you won't have to spend the evening alone."

When I burst into the house, Mona was waiting for me, dressed up, with a festive table set and candles lit.

"Show me your phone," I growled.

Mona handed it to me without any hesitation. It didn't take long to find what I was looking for. What I read shattered the last of my hopes that she was innocent. I was so furious I wanted to kill her. The woman I loved so much turned out to be a complete slut. After verbally tearing her apart, I only came to my senses when, after slamming my fist on the table, a glass tipped over and shattered on the floor. I left money on the table, wanting to insult her—after all, she was only with me for the money. Whore. Finally, I suggested she get rid of that bastard child.

As I left her for good, I told her to get lost. I knew full well she had nowhere to go. But the revenge felt so sweet. Mona begged me to listen to her, but why? why did she think I was a fool who could be deceived?

Cornelia was waiting for me downstairs. She hugged me, told me she would take care of me, and we drove to a bar. There, I drank, trying to drown my despair, anger, and pain. I drank for two days. But I couldn't go to work looking like that. So, I had to go home. I hoped she had moved out. My way home passed by the bar where Mona's friends liked to gather. The taxi stopped at a crossroads, and before my eyes, a scene unfolded that shocked me. Sitting on a stone wall was that same Jacques, with his arms around some burly biker, who then kissed him on the lips. Jacques wasted no time and wrapped his arms around the biker's neck, returning the kiss. I closed my eyes. What is happening?

The taxi moved on before I could even think about what to do. When the driver stopped at my house, I looked up at our window, but it was dark. She wasn't there.

Quietly climbing the stairs to the third floor, I opened the door and saw the food left on the table. I looked around, and nothing seemed to have changed. I sighed. Rushing to the wardrobe, I opened the doors. Her clothes were still there, but only a few. The suitcase was gone. Damn, she left. I hurried back to the living room, glanced at the table, and saw the money I had left. She didn't take it. Shit. My head throbbed with thoughts and the remnants of my hangover. I sat on the sofa and immediately noticed the house keys and her phone left on the side table. She didn't take her phone. Strange. But then I realized I had bought that phone for her myself. She left it behind.

With trembling hands, I tried to pick it up when something clinked and rolled onto the wooden floor. Bending down, I saw it was a ring. An engagement rings. What the hell? she didn't take it either. I rushed to the safe where I kept her jewellery—the ones I had spoiled her with. Opening the safe, I saw that nothing had been touched, not even the money. I sighed. Cornelia's words echoed in my head: "she's only with you for the money." but if that were true, she would have taken everything. I sat down on the bed, holding her phone. Shit, it was dead. While searching for a charger, I tried to remember if she had ever asked me to buy her anything. But I couldn't recall her ever doing that. If I ever bought something, it was only as a gift. What crap had Cornelia been spouting? Finding the charger, I plugged it in. As it charged, I prayed there would be something on the phone—maybe she left a message.

The first thing I saw was a message from none other than Cornelia: "How are you feeling, bitch? if he won't be mine, he won't be yours either." oh, shit. Oh god. Then I found missed messages from Jacques, warning her that someone was conspiring against her at the agency and that the queen was furious, claiming Mona had seduced her husband. The secretary had prepared the contract termination papers for immoral behavior and sent them to her home by courier. That's when I noticed the envelope slipped under the door. Inside were the documents—she hadn't taken them. She lost her job. Was this Cornelia's doing too? both worked at the same place. Oh god. Digging deeper into her phone, I found that she had spoken with the same agency owner. Jesus...

I sat down on the sofa, staring at the money in front of me. But then I noticed something else I hadn't seen before: a folded letter.

What I read made me cry, feel like a pathetic fool and a wretched bastard. It laid out a few simple facts. I read it for the third time:

"Jeremy,

You didn't let me explain, so I have the right to tell you the truth. Jacques is totally gay, and he was never interested in me as a woman. Remember the day you left for London? Remember how that morning I got my period, and you joked that you wouldn't need to put a chastity belt on me? And that bastard child is your child, the one you wanted. The child is not to blame for the fact that his father is an idiot. And I will never let him think that he's unwanted, the way I felt all my life.

So, when he's born, I will legally demand a paternity test because you wanted him. And I will never let him feel inferior."

And that was it. No thank you, no goodbye, no "I love you."

How can I find her now?

Now I had a goal—to corner that bitch Cornelia and get the truth out of her. But I didn't even need to force it out of her. When I arrived at her place, she didn't see me, as she was talking to someone on the phone from her balcony. She was laughing, bragging about how she ruined both of us for rejecting her, for choosing that fool over her, the beautiful one. She said I would now have neither Mona nor her. And that Mona, in her pursuit of an acting career, would surely get rid of that bastard child, now that she had no job, no home, and would never return to Lithuania. So why would she want the burden of that idiot's kid? Cornelia laughed about how easily I had believed her. And that Mona, left without money, could film cheap porn to survive since no modelling agency would ever hire her.

One thing was clear to me: Mona couldn't return to Lithuania.

Cornelia never expected me to return. So, when her sweet voice came through the automatic door speaker, saying, "how can I help you?", I changed my voice and replied, "a beautiful bouquet for Ms. Cornelia from her loving admirer." The fool opened the door, and I slipped in, grabbed her by the neck, and pinned her against the wall.

"Why did you do this?" I snarled.

She just laughed. "You shouldn't have rejected me. Did you think she was better than me? at least I loved you."

"Screw you, you bitch. What kind of monster are you, Cornelia? was it you who spread the rumours at the agency that she seduced Victoria's husband?"

"But it worked, didn't it?" she laughed. "She won't get hired anywhere now. Let her go to hell, the bitch. I was supposed to be the model, I was supposed to be noticed. And what is she? the daughter of a whore. What do you all see in her?"

"Where could she be?" I fumed.

"Where? Getting an abortion, where else. Do you think she wants your brat?" Cornelia laughed again. "Do you even realize how long she saved to escape from that dump where she lived? Bastard. Whore, just like her mother. But don't expect me to need you either. Mona should thank me. I showed her your true colours. You believed the gossip instead of your lover."

"Are you happy now, ruining your friend's life?" I asked through clenched teeth.

"Of course, I just got revenge on both of you. Now get out of my house, or I'll call the police."

I pulled out my phone and turned off the voice recording app, making sure she saw what I was doing.

"You'll burn in hell, you whore. I'll curse you every day, and if Mona does anything to my child, it'll be your fault. I'll find you and kill you with my bare hands."

She scowled.

"Don't try to scare me. I've been threatened by worse," she sneered.

"Maybe... but they didn't have the intention to kill you... Now, every time you walk down the street, turn around to see if someone's following you. Because I won't leave you alone," I said, slamming my fist into the wall near her head. She flinched. Then I turned and left.

I realized one thing: by deeply hurting Mona, I had lost her. And I had even paid for her to get rid of my child. Tears filled my eyes as I walked home blindly. Trusting a whore, I had lost them both. God, protect my little one, don't let her give up. I will find you both, and I'll crawl on my knees, begging for her forgiveness. Mona just don't give up. Everyone deserves a second chance.

In search of Mona

If you think I found her, you're mistaken. The next day, I went to her agency and let Victoria listen to the recorded conversation. With a sigh, she confessed that besides her Paris address, she had no further information about Mona. I even asked Jacques if he knew where she was. But Jacques didn't want to talk to me. He shot me a disapproving look, turned his back, and walked away. I hurried after him and grabbed his arm. Then he turned and said:

"You took my friend away from me. A wonderful person. You're not worthy of her."

"I made a mistake, I beg you, help me get her back."

"All I know is that she wrote she was flying away. No mention of where, when, or with whom. It was too painful for her to talk."

"Do you know where she lives in Lithuania?" I persisted.

"I only know it's in a small town. And that when she was born, she ruined her mother's life. Don't expect her to return. She lived in poverty for years, saving up to come here. Leave her alone and stop hurting her."

"Jacques, she's pregnant with my child, I can't just leave her."

He sighed again.

"The story repeats itself. She carried the label of illegitimacy, and now she's left alone with your child... Poor girl. She didn't deserve any of this. She was serious, responsible, and you made her fall in love, you seduced her, and then you destroyed her... No. I hate you. How will she survive in a place with no jobs and no future? and with a baby in her arms?" Jacques wiped away a tear.

I felt even worse now. All I had left was to go to the airport and beg the security chief to at least tell me if such a girl had flown, and if so, where. The chief couldn't help me with that. But I am wealthy, and he earns little. So, after ten minutes, I knew that she had bought a ticket to Vilnius, but the next day returned it and didn't leave from their airport.

It cost me another 500 euros to see footage of her leaving the airport with a man who was carrying her suitcase. They got into a limousine and drove away. I would recognize her from the back anywhere, but the man's face wasn't captured on camera. Inside me, a storm raged. Who was this man who took my woman away, and where did they go? All that was clear was that the limousine had come to pick them up. We couldn't identify the license plate either. Watching it all happen, the burning question was: who took my girl?

I was consumed by jealousy, pain, love, and despair. I hired people. We found out that the limousine was rented and that it drove from one airport to another. Did she leave with him? the driver wasn't very talkative, but he liked money. He hadn't heard what they talked about, but he guessed the man was around forty years old. The service was paid for by a transfer. And believe it or not, the payment came from the company I work for. This revelation stunned me. But the finance department had no idea who had made the payment or who had taken the car. Mona knew only a few people from my company, and they all lived here, were happily married, and were older.

I then took a drastic step—I paid a national tv channel to show her photo during the news as a missing person. I offered a great reward for any useful information. Sadly, I didn't receive a single valuable response. She had vanished into thin air. I then circulated a query through all our branches, hoping someone might know my girl. Again, no one answered.

I finally understood that I had lost her.

Erik

I was waiting for my brother at the airport. Recently, we had become like two ships passing in the night, always ending up in different parts of the world. There were still three hours left. It was late at night, and I felt exhausted after flying for hours from Tokyo. I desperately needed coffee. The café was small, not too crowded. I sat down. My attention was drawn to an impressive-looking woman pulling a large suitcase on wheels behind her. My god, her legs seemed to go on forever. A short skirt, high heels, a plaid blazer, and a small backpack on her shoulders. Her dark hair reached her waist. Through the open blazer, I could see her ample chest. Then my eyes moved higher as she approached. No, not French. Slightly almond-shaped eyes, full lips, high cheekbones. Her nose was red from crying. Only then did I notice the tear stains on her cheeks. She left her suitcase by a table and went to the bar to buy a bottle of mineral water. Holding the bottle and glass in her hands, she walked back to her seat, oblivious to her surroundings. She collapsed into the chair, closed her eyes, and the tears began to fall again. She sat there, not even opening the bottle, staring into the distance with eyes that saw nothing, continuously crying.

You know, I've seen a lot, heard a lot, and experienced even more in life. And I couldn't just sit there, watching this girl cry. I wouldn't lose anything by trying to help her. Not out of selfish motives. She was clearly young, and something bad must have happened. Alone in an airport at night.

She was, of course, surprised by my attention. She tried to brush me off. She didn't try to flirt. She was in a lot of pain, and I could feel it with every fiber of my being. When I touched her hand, i felt something I hadn't felt in a long time.

She had been hurt, she felt hopeless. Once, someone saved me—Tomas—when I was standing on the edge of madness, ready to end it all. When it seemed like life was slipping through my fingers. And now, I had the chance to help her, so she wouldn't feel completely alone in her misery.

And who knows what fate sends your way at the right moment? the more I talked to her, the more I liked her. I could see how desperate her situation was. And I decided to take a risk. What if... What if fate had sent her to me, and by helping her, I could free myself?

She was perfect for me. She seemed like a broken queen. Her walk, her appearance, her posture. Her simplicity, yet something rare that I hardly ever encountered—perhaps pride, or maybe that authenticity that draws people like a magnet.

She agreed. Very cautiously, very thoughtfully. And I guess she was so disillusioned with life that she didn't refuse my, an older man's, crazy offer. She was genuinely surprised by everything. She didn't try to seem like someone she wasn't. That authenticity enchanted me.

Of course, her pregnancy startled me, but... But after Rachel had gotten rid of our child, I had been terrified of having another. The way she crushed me... I couldn't survive it a second time. And now, with the chance to save not only her but also that little being, I didn't hesitate. If the father didn't want the child, then I would be the one to be the father that I wasn't allowed to be to my own child. And someday, if God wills, maybe she'll give birth to my child. She's still very young, after all.

I took her in as a treasure. I won't let her go. I'll give her a second chance, and maybe then, fate will show me mercy. And perhaps I'll finally be allowed to feel happiness. I already have everything else.

Mona

Everything seemed like something out of a Brazilian soap opera. The limousine stopped near the plane. I didn't have to worry about anything, just to climb the stairs into the sleek, small aircraft and settle comfortably into the seat.

"They'll bring us food soon," Erik smiled.

Just then, the pilot appeared. An alpha male type. His eyes lingered on me, filled with a desire that was almost tangible. I noticed Erik watching him as well, and the pilot winked at him.

"Have you ever flown in such a plane, miss?" the pilot asked arrogantly.

I nodded.

"I've spent a lot of time in the air lately," I responded calmly.

"So, are you a stewardess?" he grinned again.

"Oh no," I shook my head, ending the conversation and signalling that I didn't wish to discuss it further.

"We'll be taking off soon, please buckle up," he smiled once more before turning away.

I buckled up automatically, and then Erik warmed my heart with an act that made me feel wonderful. He stood up, pulled a small pillow from the overhead compartment, and leaned over to place it between my stomach and the seatbelt. For that gesture, I would do anything for him. He was protecting us.

"Thank you," I whispered.

"We have to take care of the little miracle," he smiled warmly.

"I don't know whether I want to eat or sleep more," I laughed.

"Hang in there a little longer, you'll eat soon and then you can rest."

We hadn't even fully taken off when a plate of delicious snacks was set before me. After devouring what seemed like an endless amount of food, I felt heavy and content and soon drifted off to sleep. Erik guided me to the relaxation area, laid me down on a wide bed, covered me with a soft blanket, and tried to leave before I even closed my eyes.

"Where will you sleep?" I asked, a bit worried, just before falling asleep.

"Don't worry, I'll figure something out."

"But there's plenty of room here, lie down next to me," I offered shyly.

"Will I disturb you?" he asked, hesitating.

"God, you're going to be my husband," I snorted.

"I have some documents to review first, and then I'll join you."

I remember nodding before drifting into a deep sleep.

We were woken up by the stewardess announcing that we were landing. I was quite surprised. I must have been exhausted to sleep so deeply. Erik was sleeping next to me.

"Our first night together," he laughed.

"I can't remember the last time I slept so peacefully and for so long."

"Me neither," he nodded. "Well, now you see how well we fit together," he winked. "We missed the chance to shower," he added with a quiet laugh.

"Maybe at the hotel?" I suggested.

He shook his head.

"I have a great apartment here, you'll like it. Let's hurry, we can grab something to eat before we land."

We stopped in front of a charming skyscraper. His apartment was on the top floor. Through the glass walls, I could see a stunning view of New York city. It was breath-taking. Erik pulled my suitcase into the bedroom, and I froze when I realized there was only one very large bed.

"Sorry, but when I bought the apartment, two rooms were enough for me. I only ever used it to sleep in."

"It's fine," I lowered my head. "You didn't plan on finding me back then."

"I'll figure something out, don't worry."

"Erik, I feel so safe with you," I smiled. "There's nothing to worry about."

And truly, it was a strange feeling to realize how good it felt to be near someone. His care and kindness wrapped around me, making me feel secure. I hadn't felt like this with Jeremy, not even with my own mother. Now, it felt like I had lived an entire life with Erik. Don't laugh—I'm not a gold-digger or someone who needs to be taken care of. But I liked being near him. Maybe I was too quick to let him take care of me. Or maybe, at that moment, I just needed someone who made me feel like I wasn't worthless or an unwanted child, but rather the one and only, a desired woman. Even if it was just for a short time, and even if it was a moral lie, it was still better than feeling rejected, abandoned, and humiliated. If this man made me feel that way, trust me, I would do anything to make him feel just as good with me. Life had taught me how to adapt well.

"I'm glad to hear that," he smiled modestly. "Once, Rachel told me that I was nothing, not worthy of a woman's love."

I turned, surprised.

"Maybe she's stupid?" I blurted out without thinking, then regretted it since I had no idea who Rachel was. "Oh, I'm sorry, I shouldn't have..."

He looked surprised by my response.

"Don't apologize. She's nothing to me."

"She's not only stupid, but also blind, Erik. No one has ever taken care of me the way you do," I told him softly.

He raised his eyebrows sceptically.

"Not even him?"

"Him who?" I didn't understand.

"Well, the man who..."

"Don't mention him. He left me. He..." I turned away, not wanting to spoil such a good conversation.

"I understand," he hugged me from behind.

"I'm very grateful to him; he's a good man."

"Why would you say that?" I pulled away in shock.

"How could I not be grateful when he gave me such a woman," he chuckled in that deep voice that warmed my heart.

"Stop," I blushed.

Mona

Then he showed me around his apartment. I was surprised by how modestly and masculine it was decorated. Also, there was practically no kitchen, just an impressive coffee machine.

"How do you cook here?"

"I don't. I eat out."

"Oh..." I was surprised.

"When there are so many restaurants and cafés around, there's no point in cooking, especially since I rarely live here."

"I see," I nodded.

"Are you coming to the office with me, or will you wait for me here?" he asked shyly.

"And I won't disturb you?" I asked timidly.

"No, if you can wait while I handle some business."

"If you sit me at a computer," I laughed.

"Of course, you can use mine. Let's go. After the meeting, we'll get you some clothes and food," he smiled. "Maybe not in that order."

His driver stopped at an impressive skyscraper in a reserved spot. It felt a bit strange. I tilted my head back, unable to take my eyes off the view.

"What floor is your office on?" I asked.

"We own the whole building, mona."

"What?" I was shocked. "You've really surprised me."

"It's so easy to surprise you," he chuckled, wrapping his arm around my shoulders. "Come, my queen, let me show you your kingdom."

I laughed.

Here, he was respected, admired, and unconditionally obeyed. No, he didn't act like an arrogant god. He was composed, focused, and very confident. He never raised his voice, made comments calmly, and people listened. He ran everything here. If he introduced me anywhere, it was as his fiancée. I could feel the glances, the evaluation from both men and women. I liked it. When he opened his office door, there was a plate of treats waiting on the table.

"Eat something, you're probably hungry."

"Erik, if I keep eating like this, I won't fit back into work after the baby is born. I'm a model, you know."

He turned to me, frowning.

"Mona, our child's health and well-being come first. My wife won't need to work. Taking care of money is my job. That's how my father and stepfather did it, and that's how it'll be. So, eat. How else will you carry a baby if you starve? your most important job now is to nurture them. And just look how tasty this bite is!"

He picked up a small sandwich with his fingers and fed it to me. It was delicious. "Now eat quietly, and then you can use my computer," he said, turning it on. "I'll be back shortly. If you need anything, just tell my secretary through that door."

"Erik, thank you."

"For what this time?"

I shyly looked up at him and replied, "For being here."

He hugged me and kissed the back of my hand.

"I'm glad I spoke to you that day. Rest now," he said before leaving.

My whole life now felt like a beautiful dream. I feared only one thing: that I would wake up, and when I did, it would be back in my old apartment, where Jeremy would once again impose his truth and destroy me. God, I loved him with all my heart, body, and soul. I closed my eyes as tears filled them. Why did he act that way? Didn't he believe me? It hurt so much. My heart bled again. I stood up and walked to the window. The view was stunning. As far as the eye could see, there was New York. Was this my new life? Would I become Erik's plaything? though, thinking about it, he never made me feel lesser than him. He never interrogated me, demanded anything, or asked for anything in return for what he gave me. I wasn't sure how long I stood there staring out the window before the door opened. I certainly didn't hear him enter the office and hug me from behind. When I turned around, he just wiped away the tears streaming down my face. But even then, he said nothing. Because, at that moment, words were the last thing I needed. Erik simply turned me around, pulled me close, and said:

"Mona, I can't give you the moon, but I can certainly make sure you feel happy."

I laughed quietly. He gently pressed his lips to my forehead and whispered softly:

"We have a meeting with someone. Let's go. But first, let me wipe those tears away."

Mona

He pulled out a handkerchief, carefully wiped my cheeks, and then led me into another room. The first thing I noticed were two heavily armed men standing by the door. They nodded to Erik and let us in. Inside, at the table, sat an elderly man with a balding head, in front of whom was a small black box. Behind him stood another armed man, watching our every move like a hawk. I tensed up in surprise.

"Erik, good to see you," the man greeted him, standing up and offering his hand.

"Your men are scaring my little one," Erik laughed.

"Don't take it personally," the balding man said to me, emphasizing the word "personally." "I rarely (stressing the word "rarely") leave my shop. But for Erik, I agreed to come here."

I smiled awkwardly, not understanding what they were talking about.

"Well, show us what you've got, Manuel," Erik requested warmly.

"I thought the best I have for an engagement," Manuel said, unlocking the black box with a key and pulling out a small tray lined with black velvet, filled with expensive rings. He pushed the tray toward Erik. "Here, Erik, pick the most beautiful one for your fiancée."

Something inside me froze, my muscles tensed, and I glanced at my hand, which had recently worn Jeremy's engagement ring. The pale band of skin left by the ring, kissed by the sun, was still visible. And now, once again... I closed my eyes.

But when I opened them, I realized both men were staring at me intently. My mouth went dry with surprise.

Erik looked over all the rings, then picked up one featuring a hexagonal diamond set on a simple white gold band.

"This one," he said, smiling at me. "Will it do?"

I knew full well that a diamond of that shape was insanely expensive. Spending so much just for the act of pretending to be his fiancée seemed excessive.

"Erik, it's too expensive. Something less pricey will do just fine. Don't spend so much on me."

Erik just shook his head and gave me a humble smile.

"Mona, I don't plan to propose to anyone else in my life, so this one should suit you perfectly."

"Miss, this diamond is exquisite," the balding man tried to convince me.

I sighed, wanting to tell him I could live without such an extravagant gem. But Erik simply pressed a finger to my lips.

"My bride is more beautiful than this ring," he said modestly. "Unless you don't like it, we can look for something else."

The bald man sighed meaningfully.

"No, it's perfect, it's just..."

"Put it on my account, Manuel," Erik said.

The balding man smiled, satisfied.

"Alright, Erik."

"Manuel, show me the wedding bands too," Erik added.

"Of course," Manuel smacked his plump lips in satisfaction. "Pick, Erik, this is the newest and finest." he pulled out another tray, filled with intricately designed wedding bands, arranged in pairs.

"I want something simple, but beautiful," Erik said.

"You're right, classic is always in style. Look at these," he picked up a pair from the tray. "What do you think?"

"Oh, Erik," I sighed, overwhelmed by how quickly everything was happening.

"Sweetheart, I want to make everything official as soon as possible. I don't want rumours spreading about us. Before it becomes visible," he gently ran his hand over my belly. "It's just a formality, don't worry. You have nothing to be concerned about," he murmured in my ear. A shiver ran down my spine. "We'll meet my family at Christmas, I'll introduce you to them, and right before New Year's, we'll get married."

I closed my eyes, not knowing what to think or feel. He was rushing everything.

"I don't want the media shouting to the world that I'm marrying you because you're pregnant, do you understand?"

I nodded. He was right. We didn't need that kind of attention.

"So, how do you like the rings?" he asked.

"They're beautiful," I replied quietly. Of course, I wanted to see more, but I didn't dare. Everything was up to him. Whatever they were, they'd be fine. After all, happiness isn't in the rings.

"Great, Manuel, I want them engraved and delivered to us," Erik said.

"Understood," the bald man nodded. "Well, if that's all, I'll be on my way," he said, closing and locking the box. He shook Erik's hand and mumbled to me, "Good luck," before heading toward the door.

We were left alone, just the two of us. Erik picked up the engagement ring from the table and turned to me. I froze in surprise, completely still.

"I know everything feels too fast for you, but I can't help it. I want you to feel safe and secure about your future. Mona, will you be my beloved woman? Just mine and no one else? Will you make me happy in a way no one else has? Will you trust my intentions to protect and cherish you? Will you let me be the father of your child? Will you marry me?"

A feeling of déjà vu washed over me. It hadn't been long since Jeremy, on one knee, had asked me the same thing. How I had cried with joy, believing every word he said. I covered my face in despair, as if fearing to wake up and realize it wasn't Erik asking me, but Jeremy, who had come back. But it wasn't Jeremy waiting for an answer. It was calm, quiet Erik, watching me intently, as if hanging on my every breath. I knew I had to answer him, but I couldn't bring myself to do it, feeling as if despair was choking me.

"I... I..."

"Mona," I heard his soft whisper near my ear. "I'm not him. I won't hurt you. Say yes."

I opened my eyes, accepting the truth for what it was.

"You won't change your mind?" I tried to find the answer in his eyes. "You won't leave me? because if you do... I..."

"No," he shook his head, "I won't leave, as long as you let me take care of you."

"Then fine," I sighed. "I agree."

He sighed with relief, pulling me into a tight embrace and kissing me passionately.

"You won't regret this, Mona, I swear."

I stood there, dazed, realizing I had willingly made the biggest mistake of my life. But a small part of my soul just wanted to feel that, to someone in this world, I wasn't an unwanted child, not a cheater who had betrayed a loving man, but simply a woman who needed love, warmth, and understanding. And I believed him. His calm blue eyes, modest smile, and warm hands felt like a guarantee of peace for my wounded soul.

After we finished embracing, he slipped the ring onto my finger. It was stunning, catching the light beautifully, and at that moment, I realized I was no longer thinking about how things would have been with Jeremy. Because he didn't need me anymore. The man beside me was my present, my source of joy, the future father of my child, and our future. And God knows, I would do everything to make him feel special.

"Well, we're done here. Now let's hurry. The tour bus with the guide is waiting for us downstairs."

"You made him wait for us?" I laughed.

"Isn't it his job to show you around New York?" he asked, surprised.

"But you kept him waiting," I giggled. "Hurry up, we can't keep him waiting any longer."

God, he had rented the entire bus just for us. Sitting in the second level, we enjoyed the views and listened to the guide tell the city's history, just for us.

Then we went shopping. He let me buy anything I liked. Afterward, we had dinner at a lovely Japanese restaurant and headed back to his apartment.

I didn't feel completely at ease, and the approaching night made me anxious. But it was all for nothing, as he prepared his bedroom for me, kissed my forehead, wished me goodnight, and left to sleep at a hotel. I felt a little guilty since I could have adapted to the situation—the bed was plenty big enough. Now I had made him feel unwelcome in his own home. But I was so exhausted that I just washed up and collapsed into bed.

In the morning, I woke to the sun tickling my face. I was surprised to hear noises in the apartment. Alarmed, I jumped out of bed. Who else could be in the apartment with me? worried, I opened the door and saw Erik, making us breakfast.

"I hope I didn't wake you. Good morning. Did you sleep well?"

"Wonderfully," I replied, realizing why he was looking at me like that. I felt self-conscious. I was wearing thin silk pyjamas that didn't cover much. "But you didn't have to leave. We could have shared your bed, it's wide enough. I didn't mean to make you leave..."

Don't worry, I respect you. We have all the time in the world. We'll share when you're ready. Sit down to eat, I know you're hungry.

Erik

I left her sleeping alone in the apartment, not because I wanted to, but just so she wouldn't feel awkward. I didn't want to pressure or upset her. I stayed at a hotel. I'm used to waking up early. So, I took care of our breakfast. And I really wanted to boost her self-esteem because that jerk managed to break her. I desperately wanted to show her that she hadn't lost anything by getting rid of him.

I always receive countless invitations to various events where my attendance is expected. But I rarely go. However, today I wanted to take her somewhere so she could feel the attention of others, the envy, and understand that now she is my woman, having climbed very high on the social ladder by becoming one.

And just then, I received an invitation to the Metropolitan Opera at Lincoln center, where the new season had just begun. Giacomo Puccini's "Tosca." Before that, there was a product presentation from a company I know. Of course, we wouldn't go there, but the opera would be perfect for us.

Do you know what's great about managing such wealth? Simply put, you can get anything you need whenever you want. You just have to say what you need, when you need it, and where to deliver it. It doesn't matter what day it is or what time. So, by early morning, I already had a wonderful dress, shoes, and a coat. It's easy when she's a model and all her measurements are publicly available. Therefore, I effortlessly got what I needed without even asking her.

Now, with a package of food in one hand and a package of clothes in the other, I was rising in the fast elevator with a smile on my face, because I missed her so much. But when I opened the door, I realized she was still asleep. So, quietly closing the bedroom door, I went to the dining room. I wanted to lay out the food on the plates and then go wake her up.

To my surprise, she woke up by herself and was now standing scared in the doorway: half-asleep, wearing sexy nightwear, her hair tousled, making my friend stir, and all I wanted was to take her to the bathroom and wash her with my warm hands under the shower, then wrap her in a fluffy large towel and take her to bed for a good lovemaking session. And not necessarily in that order. But unfortunately, I could only do that in the future. So, we just greeted each other. She complained that I had run away the night before. Easy for her to say. Women don't have an independent organ that thinks for itself. And sleeping next to her without touching her is beyond my strength. I was too weak for that. I wanted her just like this—sleepy, warm, and sexually tousled. And I really didn't want her to slip into her jeans, so I just said:

"Sit down, we're eating."

"Erik, I don't have breakfast," she shook her head in protest.

"How can you not have breakfast?" I didn't understand anything.

"I'm not a lark, I'm an owl. I'd rather sleep twenty more minutes than cook and eat. Besides, you understand, I must look good; I can't eat too much."

"But you're going to be a mom now, and your baby is hungry. And trust me, you need to eat breakfast to have energy for yourself and not let the baby go hungry."

"Okay, okay," she said, feeling awkward. "I'll eat some fruit, maybe that piece of meat, and that slice of cheese."

But I pulled her closer and, sitting her on my lap, said:

"Eat whatever you want; I'm not going to let you work for a while."

"But... Erik..."

"Eat," I put a cherry tomato in her mouth.

"Then you too," she said, taking a piece of meat and putting it in my mouth, her fingertips brushing my lips. "What are we going to do today?"

"I have a meeting, and you can either come with me or stay here, pamper yourself, and prepare for the theatre we're going to tonight."

"To the theatre?" she raised her eyebrows in surprise.

"To the opera. I hope you like it," I tried to guess if she liked classical music.

"I... where I grew up, there was no theatre, and where I lived, there wasn't much time for it either."

I realized that she wasn't very familiar with opera.

"That's okay. I love music, and we'll go to the theatre often."

"To be honest, I don't really understand or care much for classical music," she lowered her eyes.

"That's alright; we'll have plenty of time, and I hope I can introduce you to all that beauty."

"If that's what you want, I agree," she blushed.

"Of course," I touched my lips to her cheek. "You'll see, you'll really like it."

We visited the opera. She looked amazing. The dress fit her like a second skin. In fact, she refused to go to the beauty salon, stating that she could prepare for the evening herself and didn't want to waste my money on trivial things. I was quite surprised. But she was right. She managed to prepare herself and looked stunning. With her head held high, cold as an ice princess. And she only bestowed her unique smile upon me. To others and their gazes, she appeared indifferent. Mona listened only to me; she was only with me. And, of course, she loved "Tosca." I was happy to spend such a wonderful evening together.

Now all that was left was to convince her that my reclusive lifestyle on the island was a good choice. Rachel hated that island just because she couldn't escape it every day and spend evenings with her friends. Would Mona be able to adapt to her new life? Or would she also be horrified by such a lifestyle? I was afraid of one thing—that she would change her mind upon seeing what awaited her. But I was wrong.

Mona

I didn't expect that he had a helicopter as well.

"And how did you think we would get to our island?" Erik laughed.

Below us stretched the blue Atlantic Ocean. We left our plane in Miami and got into his helicopter, which flew us to the island. I was expecting to see a small house, maybe with two rooms, a thatched roof, a bit of sand, perhaps a few palm trees, and lots of blue water all around. But oh, how wrong I was.

First, there was a landing spot for the helicopter, then lots of greenery and a white, two-story house with a wide roof. I couldn't even imagine how many rooms it might have. Yes, there were palm trees on the island and plenty of sand. I didn't expect that. White sand, aquamarine-colored water, greenery—it was something beyond what I could have imagined, even in my dreams. This was my paradise.

The house was spotless. There didn't seem to be any unnecessary items, and everything that was there felt like it belonged to the island itself. I was enchanted.

"Mona, tell me, do you really need a social life?" he asked hesitantly.

"Me?" I laughed. "God, this is paradise, Erik." of course, if I had to live here constantly, it might get boring, but didn't you say you travel regularly?"

"Yes, I do," he smiled. "I'd be happy if you'd keep me company, as long as it doesn't become too hard for you."

"Of course, but it's so wonderful here, and for now, I don't want to go anywhere. I'm on vacation," I laughed, feeling satisfied.

"Well, great, enjoy it," he said, trying to unload the big box of food we brought from Miami.

"If you tell me where to put everything, I'll help you," I said, standing behind him and hugging him around the waist, pressing my whole body against him. "Erik, you were sent to me by God, no doubt about it," I said quietly, thinking he wouldn't hear. But he turned, hugged me, and pressed his lips to the top of my head. Words weren't necessary.

"Go look around the rooms while I unload everything. Today, you're allowed to be a guest," he said with a pleased laugh.

"I'll wait for you," I protested.

After about twenty minutes, he was already telling me how he built the house, how he designed it. How no one expected him to settle in so perfectly. And now they all want to visit, which he doesn't like at all because he loves peace and solitude.

I was surprised to find out that I had been given a separate room. I expected he would want to sleep together. But he thought otherwise and said that he wasn't in a rush and wanted me to decide when our real shared life would begin.

But that life started very quickly. He had already told me that this time of year often brings hurricanes and storms here. It rains a lot, and this will only end by December. After all, these are the tropics. I just didn't know what that would look like.

I remember well how we said goodnight in the evening, how I closed myself in my room and

Opened the window, wanting to hear the sea. I don't even remember how I fell asleep. But I vividly remember being woken up by the noise outside. The wind was raging, banging the shutters, and the curtain was billowing between the room and the outdoors. The palm tree looked like it was about to snap if the wind bent it any further. And that howling wind...

Don't laugh, but do you remember the hurricane Erwin that swept through Lithuania in January 2005? well, at that time, I was visiting Cora's grandparents with her, and Erwin tore off the roof of their house. Literally, not to mention a few trees that were broken near the house. We were still young girls. So, what I experienced in my childhood left a deep impression on me, and I developed a terrible fear of storms. And here, this wasn't just a storm—it was a hurricane. And we were on some island, where no help could be summoned in such weather. I was terrified, and all moral principles went out the window.

I didn't even realize how I ended up in Erik' room, climbing into his bed, teeth chattering from fear. He was sleeping so peacefully, completely unaware of what was happening outside. Yes, he was quite surprised to see me next to him, but I was trembling so much that he just hugged me, pulled me close to his strong body. Then, pressing a button, he lowered the external window shutters, kissed me, and said:

"Sleep, everything's fine. It's normal here."

Easy for him to say, "sleep." I was tormented by the mere thought of opening my eyes. But he, sensing how scared I was, kept stroking my body with his hand. My back, pressed against his broad chest, felt warmth and calm, and thanks to that, I didn't even notice how I fell asleep in his arms, exhausted from fear.

Erik

I woke up feeling someone crawling into my bed. When I saw a terrified Mona, all traces of sleep vanished. I didn't know she was afraid of storms. This wasn't even a hurricane, just a regular storm. I lowered the shutters, hugged her, pulled her close, and stroked her body until she relaxed and fell asleep. The truth is, I couldn't fall asleep as easily because I wanted her so badly.

It hurt.

I could smell vanilla and coconut radiating from her. With my face buried in her hair, I kissed her ear, but she was already asleep. I silently admired her. Then she turned, wrapped her arms around my neck, and murmured that she loved me. God, it felt so good to hear that.

But I fully understood that she didn't love me, and she wasn't hugging me in her sleep. Of course, it hurt to realize that. When I felt her lips on mine, I could have just gone along with it and enjoyed the closeness. But I didn't want that. I didn't want her to think of me as him. I wanted her to make love to me, not to that surrogate father figure. So, I pulled away from her and quietly said:

"Go back to sleep, it's late."

And she fell asleep peacefully. But I couldn't. Who is this jerk she loves even in her sleep?

In the morning, I was the first to wake up. I quietly raised the shutters with the remote. The sun was shining as if nothing had happened. She was sleeping next to me with her hair spread across the pillow. I admired her face and the peace in it. And I kept thinking about how to make her mine so she wouldn't think about that bastard. Then she stirred, sighed, and slowly opened her eyes. Realizing where she was, she suddenly sat up in bed, covering her face with her hands as if she were guilty of something.

"I'm so sorry..." she said, looking at me guiltily. "I shouldn't have come here, it's just..." she lowered her eyes.

"What is it?" I didn't understand.

"You see, it might sound silly to you, but I'm really afraid of storms."

"Why?" I was curious.

"One of the hurricanes tore the roof off the house in the village where I was sleeping as a child. Ever since then, I've been terrified."

"It's okay, everything's fine," I reassured her.

"And I'm sorry that... well, that I came to you at night. I shouldn't have done that. Forgive me," she said, swinging her legs over the other side of the bed.

God, so she wasn't dreaming. Oh no, I just pushed her away.

"Listen, Mona," I tried to explain.

"No need, it won't happen again," she shook her head, getting up, but I was faster and grabbed her hand so she wouldn't run away.

"Wait, you misunderstood," I tried to explain the situation to her.

Now she was watching me with frightened eyes.

"I thought you were asleep, dreaming about your ex..."

She furrowed her brows.

"That's how it was at first, until I woke up and felt you."

"See... I don't want to be compared to him or be a replacement. I want you to willingly forget him and give yourself to me."

She was watching me with furrowed brows, then, as if deep in thought, she simply said:

"I can't control my dreams. But you can help me erase him from my memory. I want you to fill my every thought. I want..."

"Are you sure?" I doubted if I understood her correctly.

"Yes, I never even thought of comparing you to him because they're two completely different things. And it will depend on you whether I'll even want to remember him."

I didn't need to be told twice. I hugged her, and we fell back into the bed together.

"Wait, I need to visit a certain place. You know, pregnancy has one downside," she smiled. "I'll be right back...

Mona

I watched myself in the mirror. He's so wonderfully sweet. And he didn't even try to seduce me all this time. I think it's time to show him that he matters to me too. I haven't been with many men, and my experience in bed isn't vast, so I'm not sure if I'll be good enough for him.

I run a brush through my hair, brush my teeth, and after one last glance at myself, I smile and nervously return to Erik. He's lying there, propped up against the headboard, smiling at me.

I stop at the edge of the bed, watching him. Without breaking eye contact, I slide the thin straps of my nightgown down from my shoulders. They slip down my arms, and the smooth silk glides over my body, falling to the floor. I stand before him, completely naked, save for my lace panties. His eyebrows lift in surprise.

I know how my body affects men. It's my tool of the trade. I've spent years modelling all kinds of lingerie. I'm a fashion model, and I know how to make men want me. I've worked with countless male photographers. I know exactly how to tilt my head, raise an eyebrow, bite my lip, extend my leg, or flash a seductive smile. It's my daily bread. But I don't need to do any of that here. I can see how much he's already admiring my body, then suddenly, he gets up, grabs me in his arms, and we fall together onto his luxurious mattress.

"You're so beautiful," he whispers, gently holding me, his lips brushing my ear.

"you're not too bad yourself," I tease, kissing his temple lightly.

I trace my fingers over the firm muscles of his arm, feeling the warmth of his body.

"I want to think only of you, feel you, touch you, and adore you," I whisper softly, making sure only him hears it. He pulls me closer, and our lips meet. He devours my lips, savouring my mouth with his eager tongue. I realize that beneath his calm exterior lies a man full of passion. We pull apart for air. Gently holding my face, as if studying me deeply, he asks:

"Can we make love fully? won't we hurt the baby?"

"Probably not," I shrug.

"Great," he says, laying me down on my back and quickly positioning himself over me. "I want to taste every inch of you," he whispers, his tongue tracing my jawline before playfully nibbling on my chin, his eyes locked on mine.

I grab his head and steal another kiss. As he frees himself from my embrace, he trails kisses down my collarbone, and his lips begin to descend. He cups my breast, lifting it to plant a kiss, then grazes my nipple with his palm, sending shivers of pleasure through me. A wave of excitement ripples through my body, which doesn't escape Erik's observant gaze. A soft moan escapes my lips like a sigh.

"They're perfect," he murmurs, gently teasing my nipple with his tongue.

I laugh softly, running my fingers through his hair, caressing his head. He purrs contentedly, moving his lips lower toward my belly button, making me arch my back in pleasure, feeling a soft tingling in my lower abdomen. A louder moan slips from my lips, bringing a devilish smile to Erik's face and a playful lift of his eyebrows. His hands slide down, stopping at my belly.

"Hello there, little one, how are you doing?" he kisses my belly, and I feel a tear of emotion slip out. Ah, these hormones.

"He's happy to have a dad like you," I say, sitting up slightly and propping myself on my elbows. He's next to me again, and we embrace. Wrapping my arms around his neck, I lie on my side. As our lips hungrily seek each other out, his strong hand trails down my back until it reaches my behind, squeezing it firmly. The sensation is so real, making me want to press myself closer to him. His erection, pressing into my belly, reminds me not to stop.

"You must be a gift from God to me," he says, gently nibbling on my ear, his other hand slipping between my legs.

"I think you're wrong—you're my guardian angel," I say, throwing my leg over his hip, wanting to feel closer to him.

A low growl of satisfaction escapes from deep within him, stirring a desire in me to feel him where that tingling sensation is growing stronger.

"Of course, why not," he laughs, sliding his fingers between my legs where it's so wet and slick. "God, did you get this wet for me?" he says, eyes wide with wonder.

I simply smile at him, my hand sliding down to the waistband of his boxers, yearning to feel him inside me.

He chuckles in that deep voice of his, pressing his lips to my forehead. He rolls onto his back, pulling me to his chest. Now, I get to admire his sculpted body. My fingers glide down his chest, lightly tracing the ridges of his muscles. I'm captivated by the v-line on men's bodies, so I find the beginning of that v and slowly trace it downward. He groans in pleasure. Through his boxers, I can see his erection, growing larger by the second right before my eyes. As I reach the waistband with the "Armani" logo, I pause to look into his eyes. He's watching me with a slightly teasing look, as if daring me to go further.

"Do you know why I find the v-line so attractive?" I ask, narrowing my eyes.

He shakes his head, signalling "no."

"It's like an arrow pointing to a great prize," I say, licking my lips, slipping my hand under his boxers to feel his hard, stone-like erection.

Erik moans, closing his eyes in pleasure. But I'm not in a hurry—I want to explore his boundaries. Like a panther, I get on all fours and press my lips against the bulge that seems eager to tear through his boxers and escape. I gently kiss it through the fabric, and he groans, brushing his hair off his forehead.

"You tease," he laughs, suddenly sitting up and pulling my head toward him.

"Armani is nice," I laugh. "But I think you're wearing too many clothes," I joke, sliding my hand under them, quickly pulling them down.

"You've unleashed the devil," he laughs, finishing undressing himself.

"That devil's not so bad once you befriend him," I say, running my hand along his length, admiring my new man.

"See anything you like?" he asks, his voice husky with desire, his eyes smouldering.

"Seeing is believing," I laugh. "But I won't know until I feel it," I tell him in a serious tone.

He laughs, laying me back down, positioning himself between my legs.

"You'll get your chance to test it soon," he grins, a smile unlike any I've seen from him before.

Grabbing his shaft, he pulls it back a few times, making sure I don't break eye contact. It's so incredibly sexy that I shiver with anticipation. I lick my dry lips. Watching me, he lets his hand glide where I'm already so wet, making me shudder with pleasure. I close my eyes, hoping that soon, soon, he'll enter me. But he seems to be savouring my desperate longing. I open my eyes, confused, wondering why he hasn't moved. He grins like a mischievous devil and asks, torturing me with anticipation:

"Well, what's it going to be?"

"What's what?" I ask, still not fully understanding.

"I'm waiting for you to ask for what you want..."

"Hm...," I reply knowingly. "I'd like two scrambled eggs with cheese, and a glass of orange juice."

"Perfect," he smiles, still caressing me.

If he doesn't enter me now, I swear I'll go wild. So, I simply lift my hips toward him, bringing him closer.

"God, woman, you're driving me insane," he growls.

"Sir, I'd like you inside me. Deep, deep inside," I laugh. "Now," I command sternly.

"Who am I to refuse?" he smirks, pushing in, and I feel myself filled.

God, his shaft is much bigger and longer than Jeremy's. All I can do is moan in surprise. Erik props himself up on his elbows, whispering softly in my ear: "I know you need to get used to me. We're not in a rush."

He plants soft kisses on my shoulder. I feel his shaft pulsing inside me, or maybe it's me, but that pleasure becomes mutual, and I shift, tightening around him, causing him to moan even louder. Unable to hold back any longer, he begins thrusting slowly, each push igniting a burning pleasure that makes me want to scream.

"Feel every inch of me, centimetre by centimetre. I'm all yours, my little one," he murmurs just as I feel the heat building up inside me, my muscles tightening.

"I'm about to finish," I manage to whisper just before the moment hits. My entire body tenses, and I cry out, "Jesus... Erik..." as warmth floods my body, and my muscles eagerly clamp around his shaft, pulsating. Erik keeps thrusting harder, and moments later, he roars, releasing inside me.

"You're mine, and only mine," he growls.

Then, a moment later, he slips out of me, and we both try to catch our breath, breathing heavily.

He puts his hand on my stomach and pulls me to him.

"God..." - I groan, closing my eyes

Erik

When she came out of the bathroom in her silk nightgown, a wave of warmth washed over me. I couldn't take my eyes off her as she slipped off the straps, and the fabric slid down her body,

Revealing such beauty to me.

It's no secret—I had already been snooping on google and seen photos of her modelling all those sexy lingerie pieces. I had seen her body before. Sure, I knew how photoshop worked. But now, nothing had been retouched or altered, and she was standing before me, very real and very alive.

My body reacted instantly. The thought that she was "my" woman filled me with warmth. After everything I went through with Rachel, I desperately needed something to make me feel like a real man again. Not for money, not out of flattery. She gave me that feeling. God, for that feeling, I could have given her the sky, the moon, and the stars.

And it felt so good with her. I didn't expect things to be so simple and exciting. Afterward, it seemed like this was exactly how it was meant to be, like life had brought us together for a reason.

"Are you disappointed?" I asked her timidly.

"Are you kidding?" she laughed. "It was amazing, I'd love to do it again," she said, turning with a look that made me chuckle, and after that, nothing could stop me.

Our life together quickly became very centered around the bedroom. I adored the intimacy, her sensuality, sensitivity, and sincerity. Every day, I found myself falling deeper in love with her. And it seemed like she liked it too.

Then we travelled. I wanted to do that, knowing we wouldn't be able to for a long time afterward. I wanted to show her our properties, the cities where we'd live, and the business, so she could get a sense of what I was involved in.

Mona was curious, and everything interested her. I enjoyed showing and explaining things to someone genuinely engaged. At times, it even felt like we had known each other for a long time, that we hadn't met under such circumstances.

Mona

You ask how my life changed after that morning?

I don't know what had happened in his life, he didn't tell me everything. But I could sense that his ex-had hurt him deeply. It only takes a single sentence for a woman to destroy a man emotionally. But to rebuild him, like a phoenix rising, it takes time. We were both licking our wounds. I knew exactly how he felt.

Living with him was easy, like being with someone who didn't judge me, didn't ask questions, or interrogate me. He was just there when I needed someone to get through the day. We were a good fit. He, too, had been an unwanted child in his family after his mother remarried. His life had also drastically changed. Erik was sent away by his stepfather to a private boarding school for years, and then university also lacked the warmth of home.

So, we both longed for something simple, our own thing, without pretension or the need to show off how great our lives were. Just him and me. And for a while, that's how we lived. A beautiful island, his attention, the sun, and the warm sea. Daily life, shared rest, new mutual interests, and a shared goal brought us closer together. When we realized that we were truly happy and could move forward as a couple, he suggested showing me our shared assets and introducing me to the cities where our business was based. So, we travelled. He explained the most interesting facts about the places we visited and showed me our company buildings. We visited art exhibitions, attended beautiful concerts, and went to the opera. We lived for ourselves, enjoying each other. It felt like a real honeymoon because we both knew I wouldn't be able to do this for much longer.

December came quietly. Jeremy had faded from my memory. He no longer needed me, and I didn't need him. I wondered if I would tell him when his child was born. Erik made it clear he would give the child his surname and consider the baby his own. I had promised him that I wouldn't wait too long before giving him his own child. I knew how important it was to him.

My body had changed significantly. Erik made me feel loved and spoiled in every way. I was getting tired more quickly, so we decided it was time to return to the island. There were two weeks left before Christmas. I knew we'd have to spend the holidays with his family. Was I nervous? Of course—it was important that they accept me into the family. After all, none of them knew I was pregnant.

We agreed not to tell anyone the baby wasn't his. They didn't need to know that. Our wedding was meant to be a surprise for them. We didn't plan anything big—just us, his family, and close friends. He even tried to persuade me to invite my mother and sister. But I didn't need that. I wasn't sure how my mother would react or whether she'd start resenting me.

After I left, we only spoke a few times, mostly when she needed money, not because she missed me. And I understood her completely. My sister was busy with work, and that weekend she had a performance at her lovely provincial theatre. I didn't argue. Let her dance.

I still feared that his parents would think I wasn't good enough for him. After all, in their world, it's customary to marry someone of equal social standing.

We bought Christmas gifts for his family, packed them in a box, and sent them to his parents' house. After that, we had a peaceful week of rest left on the island. So, without further delay, we headed there.

Erik

A week before Christmas, I also started to worry. I knew that my family might not be thrilled about her social status. But they'd have to accept it. After all, you can't bite the hand that feeds you. When my father passed away, just after I turned twenty-one, his will leave all his wealth to me. There wasn't a single word about sharing it with the new family. So, the full responsibility for the business my father left behind fell solely on my shoulders.

It wasn't easy to adapt to these new circumstances. It cost me a lot of nerves. I wasn't heartless, and even though my mother's new husband was wealthy, I didn't ignore the fact that my younger stepbrother had spent his entire life in that family, while I only saw them during major holidays. I supported my mother and took care of my brother's future. I knew he was as impulsive as his father, who would act first and think later.

After he graduated from university, I gave him a great job and a bright future. He certainly tried, though our paths rarely crossed. He managed our business in Europe. And now, I really missed him, especially since he was planning to introduce his future wife during the holidays. They had been together for quite a while.

Knowing all this, I didn't want to be caught off guard about Mona. I couldn't exactly tell them that we had only known each other for less than three months. I hated gossip and didn't bother looking up rumours about her online. But today, for some reason, I felt compelled to dig into her past.

I typed "Mona's boyfriend" into google. Pictures popped up, and I'd never been more disappointed in my curiosity than today. Glancing at Mona, who was napping in the hammock, I started to investigate her past relationships. First, I found someone named Arthur, then a couple of photos with a guy named George. But in the more recent ones, my brother Jeremy appeared, holding Mona, and looking way so happy.

My eyes widened in disbelief. Of course, he had been living in Paris for some time, and she was from there too. Paris isn't New York—of course they might have met at some party. Nothing strange about that. But then I searched for "Jeremy's fiancée," and that's when I felt sick. The photo had been taken not long ago, during our company's anniversary celebration. I closed my eyes.

I'm not a big fan of Facebook, though I have an account. Today, I logged in and found Jeremy's profile. My hands dropped as I scrolled through countless happy moments with her. It wasn't a brief fling. They'd been together for a long time. God, I felt nauseous. I closed the tab, left my computer, and headed for the sea.

I needed to get away from all this mess. My head was pounding from the tension and nerves. I couldn't figure out what I had done to deserve this. Every time I felt happy, fate would pull the rug from under me. And this time, it was Mona. My girl, my love, my hope, my future, and my happiness. God, what now? I sat on the sand, letting the waves lap at my bare feet. I stared into the distance as my vision blurred.

It had all been too good to be true. I felt so fortunate to have found her. Mona was perfect for me. Her calm and kindness had completely captivated my thoughts. I buried my face in my hands. God, why did you decide to take her away from me?

I knew how hot-headed Jeremy was. He always acted before thinking. I had no doubt that he had said something to her, regretted it later, and would soon beg for her forgiveness. And knowing mona's kind heart, she would forgive him. After all, he's the father of her child. I love my brother. I've always cared for him. It's important to me that he's happy. But is my brotherly love strong enough to sacrifice my own happiness for his? for the sake of the child, it would be the right thing to do, but... I could still be a father to his child. I'm older than Jeremy, after all.

With these thoughts in mind, I picked up the phone and called Jeremy, hoping I was wrong. After a few long rings, he answered. I hadn't even considered what time it was for him. His voice sounded a bit groggy.

"Hey, bro, where are you?"

"I just flew into New York. This time zone is killing me," he laughed, albeit reluctantly.

"We missed each other. I'm on the island."

"Damn, missed you again. They told me you were in New York."

"I was. But we'll see each other soon for the holidays."

"Mom said you have a woman," he tried to pry the truth out of me.

"Mom talks, mom knows, as always. What about your fiancée? I'm looking forward to meeting her," I said, praying it was true. But on the other end, there was a long silence.

"I don't know. I'll probably be coming alone. We had a fight," he said quietly.

"What happened?" I asked, curious.

Another long pause.

"I messed up," he said very softly. "I accused her of things that weren't true. And she just left. Can you believe it? she just vanished, disappeared like a dream."

"Maybe you'll reconcile once things cool down," I suggested, even though I knew it sounded naive.

"I doubt it. She's very stubborn. I don't think she'll even listen to me."

Stubborn? my Mona wasn't like that. We chatted about business for a bit longer, then said our goodbyes. Now everything was clear—I hadn't been mistaken. I didn't know how long I sat there, lost in thought, when I felt her hands on my shoulders.

"What's wrong? Why are you sitting here all alone, looking so worried and sad?" she asked softly, stroking my hair.

And the thought that soon she wouldn't be doing that anymore sent me spiralling into despair.

Mona

I wake up in the hammock and, after looking around, don't see Erik anywhere. Slowly, I lower my feet onto the grass and stand up. His computer is on the table, so he must be somewhere in the house. I walk through all the rooms, but he's not there. What's going on? I make a loop around the house—still no sign of him. Then I head toward the beach. Walking along the shore, I see him in the distance, sitting and staring into the horizon. Jeremy seems so lost in thought that he doesn't even notice me. But the way his shoulders are hunched and his head rests on his folded arms makes me worry. I approach him from behind but don't want to startle him. I gently place my hands on his shoulders, feeling how tense he is. He flinches, then turns to face me. For a moment, I see despair in his eyes and feel just how troubled he is. Then, he reaches out his hand to me. I take it, and he carefully pulls me down to sit on the sand between his legs. Awkwardly settling in, leaning my back against his broad chest, I rest my head and timidly ask:

"What's wrong?"

He doesn't answer, just rests his chin on my shoulder and wraps his arms around me like someone about to say goodbye, as if he doesn't want to let me go.

"It's fine," he says, but his voice is so strained that its clear things are far from fine.

"Is something wrong with the business?" I quietly ask.

He's silent again, and after a while, he sighs deeply and replies, "Everything is set up so well that even if something went wrong, three generations of our family would still live without a care."

"Then what is it?" I turn to him and press my lips to his cheek. "Do you feel sick, or is something hurting?" I ask, more worried now.

He hugs me even tighter, and I can feel the heat radiating from his body. He sighs again, loosening his grip as if realizing he was holding onto me like a lifeline.

"No..." he whispers.

"You know you can tell me anything you feel, right? I'll always listen to you. We'll figure something out together," I say softly, gently stroking his arms with my fingers.

He leans back, letting me go, but then, as if reconsidering, he embraces me again, maybe even too tightly.

"Sometimes you're just powerless..." he sighs so painfully that it sends a shiver through me.

God, maybe he's had a revelation. Maybe he's grown tired of me or changed his mind. I begin to worry. But it's best to just ask. That way, I won't torture myself for no reason. I've learned that in my life, nothing happens by chance. And those i love often to end up pushing me away. This time, it seems, will be no different.

"You... have you changed your mind? are you tired of me?" I turn to him, desperately wanting to see the truth in his eyes, whatever it might be.

I see his face tense up, then he sighs, startled by my question. Pulling me as close as possible, he kisses me and gently caresses my body, whispering in a soft, almost broken voice:

"God, where do you get such ideas? can't you see how much I need you? you are my whole world, and you two are my only real family."

As I sigh heavily, he rests his head on my shoulder.

"If it were up to me, I'd never let you go."

"I'm not planning on running away from you," I say quietly, puzzled by his words.

"I love you like I've never loved anyone in my life. Never forget that, okay?" he says in such a strange, almost haunting tone that I shiver. His voice carries so much pain and helplessness.

And so, we sit there until the sun sets.

Erik

I held her tightly, wanting to absorb the warmth of her body, her scent, so that when I lose her, I could remember her for a long time. And that feeling was burning me inside, making me think I might die. I loved my brother, and I knew well that when they see each other, they will forgive each other for everything. And then, I will become the uncle to their child, someone they'll see only on holidays. Every time I see her, I'll remember the days when I felt loved and so happy. It seems I'm not meant to be that way in this life.

I tried to put all of myself into the time we had left, so she would never forget how good we were together. I soaked in her attention, her laughter, her love, like the last drops of happiness before we part. But those days passed so quickly that silently, I plunged into such despair, thinking I might go mad.

And here we are, on our way to my parents' house. These are the last hours of my happy life, after which I have no idea how I will live without her.

Mona

I didn't understand what had happened, but Erik had completely changed. I sensed something was going on, but I couldn't figure out what.

"If you're so worried that I won't get along with your family, you should know that I'm a hundred times more terrified," I quietly told him on the plane.

"My love, I don't care what they think about us. If they don't like us, they can live without us," he laughed. "Besides, I doubt they'll say anything, since I'm the one making their life possible. I pay their bills."

"Listen, Erik, but if we see that they really don't like me... could we leave earlier?"

For a moment, I saw joy in his eyes, which quickly disappeared.

"God, I'd give anything for that," he muttered, leaving me puzzled.

But I was so nervous that my fingers went cold.

Erik took care of every little detail. When we landed, a limousine was already waiting to take us to long island. But halfway there, it unexpectedly stopped. I didn't understand why.

"I know you can't sit for too long. Let's stretch our legs," he said quietly.

We got out and walked for about half an hour through a mostly empty park. Erik was very quiet, focused, and I was afraid to break the silence with foolish questions.

"Let's go back, it's enough," he said, stopping and grabbing the fur collar of my coat, then kissed me as if he were about to go off to war and never return. "And never forget one thing," he sighed. "You are the most important person in my life. I love you with all my heart. And if I could..." but he didn't finish the sentence, turning away from me but still holding my hand. "Let's go face our fate," he laughed strangely, and we got back into the car in silence.

Everything felt like I had been dropped into the middle of a book on page 203, where the action is unfolding, and I know nothing about it, yet I'm suddenly the main character who must survive, God knows what. But I didn't dare ask, seeing how tense Erik was. I had never seen him like this. Maybe his family is strange? Or maybe their relationships are bad? but the mood was no longer cheerful. Fear gripped my bones. Erik didn't let go of my hand, and we sat the rest of the way to his parents' house with our fingers intertwined. In that uncomfortable silence, I felt like I could suffocate. The feeling that I was very important to him was much stronger than the fear that had arisen.

The house looked stunning. Against the background of yellowish walls, frosted bushes, Christmas lights, and a wreath with a big red bow on the front door, everything looked like a picture from a storybook with a happy ending.

His mother opened the door. A smile lit up her face when she saw her son, and she cast a quick glance at me, as if evaluating whether I was fit to be let into the house. I handed her the Christmas bouquet, saying:

"Merry Christmas."

She smiled warmly.

"Come in, come in, it's so cold outside."

When we entered, an older man with greying hair stood in the hallway. He was probably Erik's stepfather. He watched us with interest. Erik extended his hand to greet him. After helping me with my coat, he hung it in the closet. That's when I noticed both of their gazes fixed on my belly. I froze for a moment. His mother's face lit up first, followed shortly by his stepfather's.

"I'd like to introduce my fiancée, Mona," Erik said very calmly, wrapping his arm around my shoulders. "Mona, this is my mother, Jennifer, and my stepfather, Andrew."

I smiled shyly.

"Nice to meet you, Mona. Erik, you sneaky one, why didn't you mention this earlier?" his stepfather teased.

"I wanted to give you a Christmas surprise," Erik replied even more calmly.

"A double surprise," his mother smiled. "Congratulations. I'm so happy that you've made my son happy," she said, hugging me.

I just shrugged.

"When's our big day?" Andrew asked.

"If you mean the wedding, it's December 30th. If you're asking when your grandson will be born, that'll be in less than three months," Erik answered again on my behalf.

"A grandson?" his mother exclaimed.

I nodded.

"Oh my god, Mona. That's wonderful," his mother said, delighted. "Our family will have an heir," she giggled with joy. "It's a shame your father can't see this," she added, lowering her head. "Erik, go show Mona around the house, and we'll finish getting ready for the holiday."

Jeremy

These holidays have lost their meaning for me. My fate loves to ruin my plans. We were supposed to celebrate together with Mona, announce our engagement to my family. I was so happy. And I screwed everything up. I had even booked plane tickets to New York for both of us.

All New York was glowing, ready for Christmas. But I didn't feel like celebrating. I was just mourning the loss of my light, my love, and most likely, my child. Could anything be more heart-breaking? When the taxi stopped in front of our main office, it was snowing heavily. Well, at least I could confide in my brother. Maybe he'd understand. I didn't have anyone else. I head up to the fifty-fifth floor, shaking off the last snowflakes on my winter coat in the elevator. The elevator doors open, and Dolores, Erik's assistant, greets me.

"Hey, Dolores, is Erik in?"

"Hello, hello, traveller. You just missed him."

"He left?" I ask, concerned, frowning.

"No," she laughs, "they flew off to the island."

"They? who's 'they'?" I don't understand.

"Erik and his fiancée. He said he'd be back after Christmas."

"His what?" I was still in the dark.

"You didn't know?" she chuckles. "Such a beauty, so lovely. They make a perfect couple. Erik was practically glowing with happiness."

I nervously brush my hair back. "I didn't know. He didn't mention anything. We haven't seen each other in ages."

"It's okay, you'll see him at Christmas," she pats me on the shoulder.

Well, even that lazy guy found himself a wife. I thought he'd never get around to it. After his divorce from Rachel, he fell into depression and buried himself in work. But now... maybe it's for the best. He deserves a happy ending.

That week leading up to Christmas flew by. But the closer the holidays came, the more I felt the loss. I stayed in a hotel because I didn't want to face the interrogation at home. My parents were expecting the two of us, but things didn't turn out that way. Now, I'm driving to their place in a rented Lexus. Maybe it's for the best that Erik is bringing his fiancée. My parents will be more reserved with strangers around and won't question me as much.

My dad greets me at the door, obviously surprised to see me alone. Then my mom hurries over, giving me a hug. I kick off my snow-covered boots.

"Erik's not alone," my mom quietly says. "He brought a beautiful girl with him," she can hardly contain her excitement.

I go to say hello to my brother. As I walk into the dining room, the first thing I notice is a familiar scent that completely disarms me. I close my eyes, take a deep breath, and sigh. It smells just like her. The woman I drove away from my life. The next thing that hits me is seeing erik by the window, embracing a woman. They're both looking out. The woman is wearing a short black dress, with gorgeous long legs and black hair that looks like it's been cut with a knife. I close my eyes because the sight is so familiar. I try to steady my breathing. It's just déjà vu, I tell myself. I see her everywhere, but she's not here. On the street, in the subway...

"Hey, Erik," I greet him hesitantly.

They both turn around, and I feel like I can't breathe. It's like something's choking me. I try to catch my breath, but I can't. I'm terrified that I'm dreaming, that this is just a horrible nightmare and I'll wake up any second. Standing before me is the love of my life, her eyes wide in shock, just like mine. God, Erik is watching me like a hawk, ready to tear me apart. His hands slide down her body and rest on her now noticeably round belly. She quickly catches on to what's happening, straightens up, and leans against Erik, placing her hands on his. My eyes fixate on the huge diamond on her finger, and the sight burns through me like a knife in my gut. I close my eyes because I can't handle the feelings surging inside me. When I finally open them again, I thank God for at least one thing: she didn't have an abortion. But now, she's wearing a mask of indifference, as if she doesn't even know me.

"Hello, Mona," I say in a voice lower than usual, as it's still hard to breathe.

She trembles, her whole body shaking, and Erik presses his lips to the top of her head. Rage flares up in me because I feel betrayed by her.

"So, you ran off to him," I don't know what forces me to say these bitter words, but some inner demon takes over.

She just shakes her head as if saying "no." but my mother appears in the doorway, and Erik firmly says:

"Jeremy, not now."

I feel heat spread through my body. My tie starts to choke me. I loosen it. Did Mona run to Erik? But how? She didn't even know him; I never even mentioned his name to her. They were from different countries, different last names. We had never met with him together during those two years. When he visited, she wasn't home. Erik didn't even know her name. Something's not right here. I look up at the happy couple. Erik stands like a protective wall between them. Stuck to her like glue.

"Don't blame her, she had no idea. Neither did I," Erik's look could kill me if it had the power.

"What are you boys talking about?" my mother asks as she brings a Christmas goose to the table. "Sit down, kids, the food's getting cold."

"Jeremy, where's your fiancée?" my dad asks.

I glance at the happy couple and quietly respond to him:

"She's not coming. She left me. Found someone better," I explain, giving Mona a look full of despair. She glares at me like she wishes I didn't exist.

"But didn't you say you've been together for two years?" my mom asks, annoyed. "How could she?"

"It's my fault, mom. I was tricked by her jealous friend, and like a fool, I believed it."

"Well," my dad laughs. "You believed a stranger."

"And how do you feel now?" Erik asks, staring at me.

I just shake my head.

"Brother, my heart is breaking from the pain. My life has stopped."

"Well, at least one child in this family is smart. Look at what a beauty your brother found," my dad smiles, pleased.

The thought alone makes me feel sick, so I just nod and whisper, "He's lucky."

Erik's hand rests on her belly, gently stroking it. God, if I could do that now, I don't know what I'd give. I close my eyes, take a deep breath because it's too hard to watch another man touch the woman I love, even if that man is my brother. But then I start to wonder—could the child be his? what if Mona got pregnant with Erik's child and lost mine? After all, you can't pin someone else's three-month pregnancy on another man. God, what if my child is gone? Erik's every move shows that Mona is his. I wipe the sweat from my forehead with the back of my hand and try to catch Mona's gaze. But to her, I don't even exist. She's ignoring me, and she's doing a great job of it. Meanwhile, Eric is feeding her the tastiest bites, and Mona is rewarding him with her beautiful smile. I swallow hard. I can't even eat, even though I'm sitting at a table full of delicious food. I push the food around on my plate with a fork, while my mind is far away from here.

"And you know, in three months, their son will be born," my mother says to me. "Isn't that wonderful?"

The fork slips from my hand and crashes loudly onto the tiled floor.

"Are you okay, Jeremy?" my mother asks.

"I'll be right back," I say nervously, standing up from the table, unable to sit there any longer. I rush to the bathroom and close the door. It doesn't take a genius to figure out that it's my child. My son, whom Erik is now presenting as his own. Damn it. I lower the toilet seat and sit, holding my head in my hands. God, help me. How do I win her back now when she's in Erik's arms? He's a billionaire, and I'm just a foolish betrayer who threw her out of my life. I can't stand seeing him caress her, seeing how devoted she is to him, how happy they both are. I can't let everyone believe that this is Erik's child. He's mine. My son. I stand up and turn on the cold water, splashing it over my face to wash away the sweat. Focus, Jeremy, you must apologize to her, you must win her back. She's your woman, and that's your child.

I return to the table. The conversation is already in full swing.

"Where did you two meets?" my father asks them.

"At the airport," Erik smiles. "That day, her beloved man betrayed her. I couldn't stand to see someone suffering like that."

"Oh my," my mother sighs.

Erik glances at me, then presses his lips to the top of her head.

"She felt like she had lost everything. I had nothing left to lose. I was captivated by her," he lifts her hand to his lips. "A little compassion. I admired her sincerity and authenticity. Plus, she's a wonderful woman, and I liked her from the very first moment. Everything happened naturally after that. And here we are together."

God... So that's how they met. I lower my head, unable to look at them. I'm choking on pain, despair, and jealousy.

"The lord works in mysterious ways," my happy mother sighs. "But you two have brought so much joy to this house."

I get lost in my thoughts and don't even notice when my mother starts talking about how calm Erik was as a baby, and how maybe his child will be the same. I can't hold back any longer.

"Mom, that child is mine," I say very clearly to them.

Everyone at the table falls silent and stares at me as if I'm the last fool on earth. The silence is so thick, I feel like screaming.

"And Mona is my fiancée," I say even more quietly, afraid to look at her.

"What are you talking about, Jeremy?" my father snaps at me.

"I'm the man who betrayed her. I have no idea how they met at that airport," I dare to look at them.

Mona turns pale. All eyes are now fixed on her.

"I don't understand anything," my mother says.

"I was misled by her jealous friend. I believed her, got insanely angry, thought that Mona had been unfaithful to me, and that the child wasn't mine," I say, standing up, putting all my hope in her kindness and love, praying she'll forgive me.

Then, walking around the table, I kneel at her feet, grasp her trembling hands, and look into her eyes as I confess everything.

"Mona, my love, you have no idea how happy I am that Erik found you. Erik," I look at my brother and see panic, horror, hatred, and something else in his eyes, but I don't care anymore. All that matters is winning her back. "Brother, I'm so grateful to you for taking care of her when I lost my mind. My love, you know how much I love you, and when that snake Cora told me the child wasn't mine, I thought I would go crazy."

She pulls her hands out of my grasp and even recoils from me, leaning back into her chair.

"And I'm also so grateful that you saved our baby," I thank her, watching as her expression changes from indifference to one full of hatred.

"And why wouldn't she have saved him?" my father asks, curious.

I don't know how to answer him. I even shudder when she responds:

"Yes, Jeremy, why don't you tell me why I should have saved him?" she asks so coldly that chills run down my spine.

"I..." I stammer, unsure how to explain to my parents.

"Go on, tell them, everyone's curious," Erik says to me.

I realize I won't be able to get out of this unless I tell the truth.

"I didn't believe he was mine," I say, lowering my head.

"And?" my father asks, leaning forward over the table.

My tongue feels heavy, and I can't bring myself to say it. I feel so guilty. The silence is suffocating, making me feel nauseous. Then Mona's cold laughter pierces the air.

"Why are you quiet? You told me yourself that the bastard wasn't yours."

Silence again.

"I made a mistake, Mona."

"You made a mistake saying that, or paying me to get rid of him so you could move on with your life?"

The silence is broken by my father's voice.

"What did you do?" my father asks as he stands up from his chair.

Now I want to sink into the ground.

"I left her money so she could get rid of him."

"Why would you do that?" I hear Erik's soft voice.

"I wanted her to feel as much pain as I did when I thought she had cheated on me."

"And did she?" my mother asks.

I shake my head like a guilty child.

"No, her friend made up the story to get back at Mona for choosing me. And at me for leaving her to be with Mona."

"Well, have you figured everything out?" Erik asks me coldly.

"I'm not to blame, I was misled..." I try to explain.

"You clearly told her the child wasn't yours, Jeremy. So that's where we'll end it," he sighs.

"He's mine, Erik. She's the woman I love."

"Alright," my father sighs. "It was a misunderstanding, Erik. But thank God the baby is fine, and so is the mother. Erik, you're a smart and mature man. You understand that Jeremy deeply regrets his actions. You've always loved your brother. You can't destroy what's already been united by God. Mona, can you forgive Jeremy? After all, it's Christmas."

I can't take my eyes off her. I only see her eyes, but her thoughts are far away from here.

"Forgive me, my love, I can't live without you both," I beg her.

Erik stands up from the table and leaves. She covers her face with her hands and remains silent.

"Mona," I try to reach her heart.

She takes a deep breath and says:

"I forgive you."

I see Erik standing in the doorway, waiting for her response. Sighing deeply, I grasp her hands again, kissing her fingers. Then, as if waking from a trance, she suddenly remembers Erik, looks around, and not seeing him, jumps up from her chair and frantically looks around the room, searching for him.

"Mona, where are you going?" I try to stop her, but she rushes off.

Mona

Erik and I were admiring the frost-covered plants in the garden when I heard a familiar voice. It felt like electricity jolted through me. A wave of terror gripped me so tightly that it seemed my heart would stop. We both turned around at the same time. And there he stood in all his glory—Jeremy, looking lost. I saw only his eyes, filled with surprise and fear. He didn't expect to see me here, just as I didn't expect to see him. Jeremy froze instantly, even stopped breathing, but then he regained himself and greeted me. But I couldn't say a word. What could I say to him? He had already told me everything, trampled me into the ground, humiliated me, and discarded me like used trash. So, I remained silent. Then he laughed and reproached me for running off to Erik. I shook my head in protest, but once again, my tongue wouldn't move. My mouth was dry as a desert. But then their parents appeared, and Erik cut off Jeremy's ramblings.

We sat down at the table, and with all my strength, I tried to imagine that he wasn't there, that it was just a bad memory, and that the only man in my life was Erik—the man for whom I would do absolutely anything. I could hear talk somewhere about how Jeremy had broken up with his fiancée, but my head was ringing so loudly that it felt like everything was happening somewhere far away, not to me. I was too afraid to even move.

Jeremy couldn't take his eyes off me—off my belly—and I could only imagine what he was thinking. Erik, as if understanding what was happening, didn't move his hands from my belly, trying to protect us, and I was deeply grateful to him for that.

His mother proudly told Jeremy that soon our son would be born. And then I saw such pain on Jeremy's face that he dropped his fork to the ground and, jumping up from his chair, made an excuse before hurrying away from the table.

The news hit him hard. Was it because I was carrying his son? Or because the family had accepted the child as Erik's? I couldn't think logically anymore because that thought hurt me even more. "Whore... You think I'll raise your bastard?" I could hear his words again in my ears, words I had almost forgotten with time. I felt sick from the stress.

I couldn't even focus on what Erik was saying about how we met. My thoughts drifted to our little apartment in Paris. I saw the money, remembered my suitcase, and the horror of saying goodbye to the happy life I once had. All I wanted was to disappear from this house and be on our island, safe in Erik's strong arms. I needed nothing else but him.

What happened next, I least expected. Erik announced to everyone that I was his fiancée, and the child was his. I was seized by such fear that I could barely breathe. I didn't even know if it was a second wind kicking in or a mother's instinct to protect her child. I lashed out at him with words, not knowing if I was trying to defend myself or make him feel the same pain I had gone through.

He pleaded, he begged, his eyes filled with tears, and he knelt on the ground... I tried to understand what I felt for him. If only he had said those words back in Paris... Maybe then... Maybe I would have believed him. But now, the man kneeling before me—he was someone I felt nothing for. No love, no respect. Nothing. And I didn't even know if I believed his words.

Then I heard Andrew's voice, saying it was Christmas and I should forgive him. Jeremy regretted his mistake, claiming he had been deceived. I closed my eyes and realized that even back when he swore, he loved me, when he promised to marry me, he hadn't believed in me. He hadn't believed in my love, my loyalty, or my feelings. He had immediately trusted some random girl he had known for just a few weeks. And suddenly, everything became clear to me. I had nothing in common with Jeremy. And all this talk was hurting the man I truly loved. It was as if I awoke from a long stupor. I tried to end this charade:

"I forgive you," I said, only because I didn't want to discuss it any longer.

When I turned toward Erik, I saw that he was gone. Jesus, I screamed in my mind, and rushed after him.

"Mona where are you going?" Jeremy tried to stop me, but I was already running, not wanting to answer him.

Erik

This was to be expected. He admitted his mistake, and she forgave him. I knew this would happen. I stood up because, after my stepfather's declaration of how I should behave, I couldn't stay there any longer. I needed to get out of there as quickly as possible. To sink into silence, pain, loneliness, and somehow try not to break. I felt nothing anymore. It hurt so much. There was no more justice in life.

God, Mona, how much I love you. I love you so much I could die for you. And if you'll be happy with him... If you... I'll let you go. I swallow the pain, the despair, grab the suitcase handle, and start throwing things into it when the door opens, and Mona rushes in with wild eyes.

"Erik..." she whispers.

I can't look at her because I'll break down in front of her.

"It's okay, my love," I tell her. "Don't explain, I understand you."

"Erik..." she says even quieter, but with such pain in her voice.

"Don't worry, sweetheart. I'll take care of your financial situation. You'll still be able to visit that clinic, and even give birth there if you want. Nothing will change, except..." I stop because it's so hard to speak.

"Where are you going?" she asks quietly.

"Well, you see..." I answer her even more softly. "I..."

"So... So, all we talked about... All we dreamed of..." she sits on the far edge of the bed, turning her eyes toward the window.

"Mona... Please don't..."

She now turns, wipes her tears from her face, and says even more quietly:

"So, you're leaving me too..."

I don't understand anything, I just stare at her.

"Mona..."

She suddenly jumps up from the bed and shouts:

"Don't, Erik. You didn't need to lie to me or promise me anything. I didn't know he was your brother. I swear, I didn't know," she sobs, covering her eyes.

Now I'm even more confused.

"Mona," I rush to her and embrace her.

I try to breathe in her scent. But she pushes me away with all her strength. The door to the room opens, and my entire family stumbles in.

"Mona," Jeremy shouts, though it's unclear whether he wants to pull her away from me or embrace her himself.

"What?" she shouts angrily. "What do you want from me?"

Everyone falls silent, watching the scene unfold.

"Come with me, let's let Erik leave," he really tries to pull her away from me.

"What are you talking about?" she retorts, stepping away from him.

"You forgave me," he pleads.

"So what?" she frowns, planting her hands defiantly on her hips. "You already paid me for my efforts to please you over those two years, even a thousand euros. Of course, some of that was for the abortion. Tell me, Jeremy, what do you need with a whore?" she starts laughing. "Did you think I'd come back to you so you could humiliate me again at the first opportunity?"

Jeremy watches her, pale. My father, eyes wide open, tries to understand what's going on.

"You know, the day you ordered me to get rid of your son, you killed me too—my feelings for you. You betrayed my love, my trust in you, and made me hate you. And if you think you can win me back with your snivelling apologies, you're dead wrong. You don't know me at all," she laughs again.

Jeremy leans against the wall, his whole-body trembling.

"But you forgave me," he whispers.

"Yes, I forgave you because I realized you mean nothing to me. I forgave you and buried you in my mind. And that child," she pokes her belly with her finger, "belongs to this jerk," she points to me, "who promised to marry me, but now is running as far away from me as possible. And you know why?"

But I don't let her finish.

"Mona, stop."

I try to pull her close to me, but she resists. I'm stronger, though, and when I embrace her, I kiss her passionately. Mona stands there, stunned, mouth wide open. She wipes her lips with the back of her hand and says:

"You have two minutes to explain yourself," she frowns.

She's so beautiful when she's angry. I feel an urge to lay her down and give her a good spanking to drive all those bad thoughts out of her head. I release her from my embrace, letting her regain her composure.

"My love, I thought that after forgiving him, you'd stay with him. Unable to bear it, I wanted to run away as fast as possible."

"God," she sighs, and I see her become weak.

But Andrew notices it first and catches mona with his strong hands, trying to keep her on her feet.

"Leave the mother of my grandson in peace, everyone. Open a window, she needs air."

Jeremy rushes to the window, and I take Mona from my stepfather and lift her in my arms. I carry her to the bed and lay her down carefully. Sitting beside her, I hold her hand and speak softly.

"Without you, every sunrise and sunset lose its beauty. Without you, my life has no meaning. Without you, I won't be able to live a single day. I love you so much that I would conquer all your fears and mine, just to make you happy. And there's nothing else I want more than to spend the rest of my life with you."

"God…" she whispers softly, wrapping her arms around my neck.

I don't even notice when everyone leaves the room, but I hear Andrew tell Jeremy:

"Fool… But at least my grandson will stay in our family."

"So, you're going to marry me?" she asks, doubting, still in my arms.

"Yes, and I don't think I'll be able to wait until December 30th," I laugh.

She chuckles.

"God, I'm so hungry I could eat a horse," she laughs.

And we return to the table. In the doorway, I stop to kiss her. She looks at me, surprised, her eyes asking "what?" I point to the mistletoe hanging above. She just laughs.

I return to the table so happy, so certain of my future. And I like it. We exchange gifts. She receives the smallest box, curiously unties the golden ribbon, and pulls out a gold bracelet with charms. She looks at me, surprised, and I explain:

"This is our story: a tiny airplane—that's the airport. A palm tree—that's our island. The blue baby booties—the moment we found out we were expecting a son. The Christmas ornament—that's our first Christmas. And the heart with a ruby—that's my heart, which will always belong to you no matter what. I love you, Merry Christmas." I embrace her and kiss her passionately.

"No," she shakes her head. "The greatest Christmas gift is you, Erik."

And we hug as if there's no one else around. Just her, me, and our baby. And then I feel a tiny foot press against my hand, resting on her belly.

From now on, I adore Christmas.

The end

Don't miss out!

Visit the website below and you can sign up to receive emails whenever Silence in the Storm publishes a new book. There's no charge and no obligation.

https://books2read.com/r/B-A-MMDQC-LMRDF